Please turn the page for more reviews. . . .

"POWERFUL . . .

In Thomas Mistler, Mr. Begley has created the perfect rendition of the postwar American patrician." —*The Washington Times*

"*Mister's Exit* is crafted with [Begley's] usual skill and grace. . . . The great appeal of his work is its elegant, understated way of penetrating the mysteries of ordinary sorrows." —*The Baltimore Sun*

"Extraordinary . . . Not since Henry James rendered the lives of Americans in New York and abroad has any writer so faithfully captured the ambitions of Harvard-educated, board-sitting executives in Manhattan as has Louis Begley. . . . The greatness of Begley's prose is its disarming elegance. . . . One wishes . . . that a novel of such exacting standards and brilliant perceptions would have no end, no matter how well it finishes." —*The Financial Post*

"At a time when many critically acclaimed books such as Thomas Pynchon's *Mason & Dixon* and Richard Powers' *Gain* are stuffed with information . . . Louis Begley's *Mistler's Exit* comes as a refreshing relief. Begley's slim novel . . . is serious and accessible, not to mention terribly funny. . . . *Mistler's Exit* can be read on many levels: as a morality tale, an absurd mystery or a critique of personal faith. In any case, it is engaging, and it reminds the reader that if life is anything, it is one's own." —*St. Petersburgh Times*

"This novel of mortality and sexuality, of remembering and reconciling, is ultimately, and ironically, affirming. It testifies to a simple but usually disregarded lesson: that it is better to live fully and die before one's time than to never really live at all." —*Booklist*

"There is perhaps no more worldly novelist writing today than Begley: worldly in his attention to class, wealth, and sex, but most of all in his attention to pleasure in the face of death. . . . Even amid the palazzos and great churches of his vividly conjured Venice, Begley displays the bitter moral intelligence, the fear of emptiness, that has distinguished his late, extraordinary career from the start."

—*Publishers Weekly* (starred review)

MISTLER'S EXIT

Mistler's Exit

LOUIS BEGLEY

Fawcett Books
The Ballantine Publishing Group • New York

A Fawcett Book
Published by The Ballantine Publishing Group

www.randomhouse.com/BB/

Library of Congress Catalog Card Number: 99-90624

ISBN: 0-449-00422-8

This edition published by arrangement with Alfred A. Knopf, Inc.

Book design by Min Choi
Cover painting: *The Miracle of the Cross That Has Fallen into the Canale di S. Lorenzo* by Gentile Bellini. Accademia, Venice, Italy. Cameraphoto/Art Resource, NY

Manufactured in the United States of America

First Fawcett Trade Edition: November 1999

10 9 8 7 6 5 4 3 2 1

For Anka, always

Ce que les hommes vont perdre, tant pis; ils ne s'en apercevront pas. Tout finit bien puisque tout finit.

—CHARDONNE, Demi-Jour

MISTLER'S EXIT

[I]

I UNDERSTAND, said Mistler.

Really, there was no need to rush the conversation. The waiting room was empty. Bill Hurley had become Mistler's family doctor fifteen years earlier, succeeding to the practice of an uncle, who died on the tennis court of a ruptured aneurism upon double-faulting in the fourth game of the fourth set of his club's senior doubles championship, when the score was forty—love. By now, he was also a friend. The secretary had specifically asked Mistler to stop by toward the end of the afternoon, when Dr. Hurley would be through with other patients. Just the same, as soon as Mistler arrived, she began to apologize, because the doctor was running late.

Don't worry, he told her. For once, I don't mind waiting.

That was the truth. An interval of empty time seemed vastly preferable to what would follow. In fact, if there was a reason to hurry, once Mistler had reluctantly abandoned a two-year-old issue of *Glamour* and found himself in Hurley's office, the place where Hurley interrogated and decreed, the reluctant flesh having been poked and kneaded into yielding its secrets in the adjoining cubicle that housed the examination table and a reliable scale, the only piece of Hurley's equipment Mistler was fond of, it had to be that the place was so ugly. With its stacks of manila envelopes containing, Mistler supposed, X rays and EKG tapes, apparently untouched since the time of Hurley's uncle (if indeed either the uncle or the nephew had ever examined their contents, which Mistler was not ready to take for granted), the fake antique desk, small enough to fit in a college dormitory room, cluttered with pharmaceutical company doodads, and, on the walls, prints of ducks alongside diplomas that traced Hurley's progress from his New Jersey prep school through the last board certification, this room spoke of indifference and small economies. One would not have tolerated such a thing in any other high-priced service business. Did it ever occur to doctors to have discussions that broke the patient's heart outside the office, over a cup of coffee, or a drink, if they were unwilling to spend money on furniture? One could, after all, with a minimum of skill, maneuver the patient into paying the check, or bury the disbursement in the statement as a stool test or the like. Most lawyers Mistler dealt with would have considered either a lead-pipe cinch.

Apparently, there was nothing further Bill Hurley intended to say without being prompted. It was up to Mistler.

All right. How much time do I have?

For what?

Before I die, of course. What else could I mean?

You could mean before we get to work. As Mel Klein told you, it may be possible to deal with this thing surgically. Right away. It's a primary cancer. That's the good news. Then, provided all goes well, you may also have treatment. That will be up to Mel. Ultimately, you would wait for a graft. They do become available.

But he also said that Dr. Steele thought the odds for this sort of operation weren't good. Have you or Dr. Klein or Dr. Steele changed your minds?

No. The growth is large and it may have spread. Dave Steele can't be sure until he opens you up.

And if it has spread?

He'll sew you up and we'll do our best to keep you comfortable.

In the hospital?

At first. And probably at the end as well. Hurley's face remained cheerful.

I think I'll pass. Can you make a guess about how long I have if I do nothing? I'd also like to know how bad it's going to be.

It all depends on what is really going on inside you. If the problem is still local, but you have no treatment, not even radiation to shrink the growth, perhaps half a year. Perhaps less. Of that time, the next couple of months should be only annoying. No worse than that. You'll become more tired and more anemic, and you'll lose weight. Later, you'll be in the war zone, especially if other organs are colonized. Every day, this will become a stronger possibility. But even without surgery, X rays and chemo could buy you time. You'd want to talk to Mel about that. Of course, if there is already general involvement, all bets are off. These things don't run on time, like Mussolini's trains. Heh! Heh! You know that.

But surely you will arrange matters so that I don't make it into the war zone as you put it. I count on that.

If you mean to suggest that I'll kill you, I can tell you right now I won't. I am here to treat patients. Of course, it's your right to refuse treatment. You will get all the medication you need for pain, but don't kid yourself. There comes a point at which medication can't do the job.

Is that any worse than what will happen if I have the operation and the treatment?

There is a chance that the growth hasn't spread and can be taken out. Then, with treatment and luck, you could lead a normal life—especially if you get a graft. Otherwise, you're right, the outcome will be much the same.

Except that I will have had the operation and the treatment and everything that comes with it. I think I'll leave matters as they are. If you could just prescribe whatever you think works best to give me a boost—vitamins, wild ginseng, tonics. I imagine that's possible.

Hurley scribbled busily. Here, he said, these may do some good and certainly won't do any harm. Then he gave Mistler the manly but affectionate look he normally reserved for telling him to cut down on red wine and shellfish, if he didn't want another gout attack, and, of course, on cigars, and continued: You shouldn't take that sort of decision before you talk it through with Clara and Sam. If you make the effort to fight, and bring them into it, they will find it easier to accept the outcome. It's extremely hard to watch a husband and father pass away—especially when it might be much sooner than necessary—because he has decided to die without letting his doctors treat him.

But it's not me making the decision to die this way and at this time—in fact quite a bit sooner than I expected. His Majesty Mistler's body made that choice. I am only deciding how I will spend the next few months. If I can help it, it won't be on hospital gurneys attached to machines that make noises like something out of a science fiction film. I don't believe Clara or Sam would like that either.

You'd be astonished. The whole world loves a fighter, your family included.

I've done my share of fighting, Bill. Believe me. Maybe that's why I am so sure that now is the time to surrender. Unconditionally!

You did promise you would bring Clara in.

Mistler took note of Hurley's increasing annoyance.

And so I will. Just give me a little time. Let her have a couple of carefree weeks. There is nothing to participate in, after all, not right away.

After that, he managed a nice smile and shook Hurley's hand.

Six o'clock already? His driver, who was waiting on Seventy-first Street, saw him, got out of the car, and stood by the door.

Thanks, Vince. I'm not returning to the office, and I'll walk home. Please call Miss Tuck and tell her not to wait for me. And would you pick me up at the apartment at eight. I'll be going out to dinner.

Spring had snuck up on Mistler, the days suddenly so long that he looked at his watch again in disbelief. Heading west toward the park, he strolled past the shops specializing in wares for the bedridden and the lame, and bars that would fill up later with hospital nurses going off duty, medical students, and interns. It was astonishing how clean the city looked. In the side street, dogs had been respecting the borders of narcissi and pansies encircling gingko trees. Tall yellow tulips sparkled spotlessly on the island that divides Park Avenue. When he reached Central Park, he gasped at the cherry and plum tree blossoms. It was a pity to have missed such a long series of weekends in the country. One lost touch with everything in nature, even the phases of the moon. The season was slower there, but he supposed that the tulips and forsythia at Crow Hill were at their best. Next year, he would get Clara to manage their social engagements in the city better and slow down his own pace. It wasn't really necessary to agree to meetings on Saturdays or Sundays, or, if they couldn't be moved, to go to them himself. Other people could attend in his place. Then he remembered the program Bill Hurley had announced. It was clear that finding time for Crow Hill was not to be a long-lasting concern. Preposterously, unmistakably, he began to rejoice. The horizon would no longer recede. The space and time left to him were defined; he had been set free.

Free from what? The question, which he immediately put to himself, had implications that were puzzling, since Mistler considered himself a happy man, as the world goes. In interviews, and in statements he had prepared for the big college reunions, he had gone on record with the belief that he had managed his life well. He considered himself entitled to that point of view, although it rested on a premise he kept secret to avoid being teased: that he was actually a self-made man, and his successes largely independent of the circumstance, in itself quite pleasant, of having been born some sixty years earlier, in the hospital adjacent to Bill Hurley's office, with a silver spoon stuck firmly in his mouth. No, there was nothing from which he should wish to escape. His marriage had long ago become tranquil. He loved his only son. Unlike Peter Berry, the cousin and former best friend whom he had forced out from Mistler, Berry & Lovett—an ugly piece of business he was close to regretting even if, in truth, it was overdue, and unlikely in the end to matter much to Peter, who would probably be just as happy raising his Morgan horses full-time—he enjoyed his work as much as ever. Peter and he had founded Mistler, Berry when they were barely thirty, giving up jobs they had gotten directly after military service in what was then New York's largest advertising agency, really huge according to the standards of that time, and prosperous and influential enough for men not quite so fastidious in such matters as Mistler's father to find working there perfectly respectable. That gentleman, himself the reigning senior partner of a Wall Street investment bank with roots in eighteenth-century Philadelphia, held all advertising and public relations to be a racy activity, fit for vulgarians and wastrel sons of his less desirable acquaintances. In fact, the senior Mr. Mistler bore some responsibility for his own otherwise quite irreproachable son's having chosen such a line of work. It paid him back for needling his son about remittance men with writer's block marooned in Paris or on a Greek island. As he had put it, it was a matter of principle, not money: Mistler family trusts, over which he exercised discretionary powers, had not been established to support dilettantes or would-be littérateurs waiting for inspiration. If his son Thomas wanted to scribble at night, that was his business, but, until he had established himself, he might as well have some recognizable occupation and discipline during the day. He liked to point out that Wallace Stevens, whom the elder Mr. Mistler counted among his friends, had never resigned from his position at the insurance company. All this was discussed calmly, and neither the father nor the son found it useful to advert to the fact that enough money flowed to Thomas from his mother's side of the family to finance just the sort of existence the senior Mr. Mistler deprecated. Thomas had enough doubts and suspicions of his own to make him fear the caprices of the Muse. A job on Wall Street seemed out of the question, downright silly unless he was to occupy the position in his father's bank which was his birthright. Its availability had been made clear. But he didn't want to work for his father. The prospect of correcting other people's manuscripts in a publishing house was even more unattractive. A man called Barney Fine, Mistler's classmate but several years older because he had been in the war, whom Mistler had known on the *Harvard Advocate,* was a copywriter in an advertising agency. Barney claimed it was the best deal in town: he was paid good money for making up jingles about soap during the day. The jingles didn't clutter up his mind or interfere with writing poetry at night. Besides, if one was good, it wasn't hard to get leaves of absence. Why couldn't Mistler do the same? He would be glad to recommend him. It was a fine plan: it seemed to Mistler he should be able to turn out copy on the virtues of hand cream and laxatives at least as well as the next part-time aesthete. He would scribble in the evenings, spend weekends holed up in the cottage abutting the lawn at Crow Hill, where a good many Mistlers and Abthorps were buried, which his father had given him as a graduation present, and enjoy his holidays or, by God, those fabulous leaves of absence in a whitewashed house on some rock in the Aegean. Peter Berry really needed to make a living. He asked Barney whether Peter might be squeezed in too.

No one was more surprised than Mistler when he discovered, right away, that he liked advertising. Three years later, he came to the conclusion that he would have even more fun if he worked for himself. It was just as well, since by then he had other reasons for showing that he could excel at running a business. He talked Peter Berry and Harry Lovett—the latter badly needed for his maturity and experience to reassure potential clients—into joining him. Harry was the big agency's vice-chairman, but had realized, as most vice-chairmen do sooner or later, that he would never become chairman, and was sore about it. Like Mistler, he had money; better yet, his money wasn't locked up in trusts. Peter came along for the ride. It seemed only natural. A New England gypsy—that's how Mistler described a character he had made up with Peter in his mind in the novel he had published the previous year; a young man less drearily circumspect than the protagonist, ready to do everything or absolutely nothing. Mistler and Harry planned to keep the agency afloat, living themselves on bread and water if necessary, for five years. As it turned out, the firm had more than forty employees and an office in London when the fifth year was up, but Harry Lovett had already died of a heart attack in his box at the Metropolitan Opera, during the second act of *Die Walküre*.

The family link between Peter Berry and Mistler wasn't much, Peter being only the son of a cousin of Mistler's mother. They had become friends at college, competing as freshmen for the *Advocate*. The following year, they began to room together. Each of them intended to write the next great American novel. It is possible, the views of the senior Mr. Mistler notwithstanding, that the cause of literature would have been better served by a life down and out in Paris or Athens. Peter had started a collection of short stories in college and worked on them in the navy. They remained in their tin biscuit box. Mistler did finish his novel, just as he had intended, but received perfunctory reviews, of the "here is another story of disorder and early sorrow in a New England prep school" variety. In truth, Mistler couldn't disagree. His novel lacked both ambition and vigor. He had hoped, though, for some sign of encouragement—even sympathy—from the one or two college friends whose first novels had also appeared recently and had been better received. Instead, it was colleagues at the agency and lackluster acquaintances who asked for inscribed copies and assured him they would read his "great work" during the next holiday. Never mind: fate had not condemned him to eat his heart out writing.

When Harry Lovett died, Mistler and Peter Berry decided to keep the firm's name intact; they would function as a duumvirate. Quickly, the impossibility of staying on the same rung of the ladder as Mistler became evident, but Peter didn't challenge him and didn't leave. And thus, before he was thirty-five, Mistler became the agency's autocrat, and he continued as such not because of his large number of shares in the company but because, beyond cavil, he was, by a long shot, better and tougher than anyone else there. Including, alas, Peter Berry. It wasn't simply Mistler's gift for the winning word, image, or campaign. He knew how to mesmerize or browbeat the most obdurate clients, and he picked the right time to expand the firm overseas and in the U.S., without allowing the character of its work to change. The press began to refer to the ineffable Mistler element, a style of advertising he had invented. From Madison Avenue's wonder child, he turned into an international star.

Then why such elation about being consigned to the rectangular hole that would in a matter of months be dug in the succulent soil of Crow Hill immediately to the right of his mother and father? Perhaps there was no explanation. If one had to be found, it appealed to Mistler to think that his unconscious, racing ahead, or through a premonitory sifting process that began when Dr. Klein, the oncologist, told him he didn't like the activity revealed by the scan of his liver, may have taken stock of the situation, and concluded that, if Klein's hunch turned out to be right, most of the problems to which he had devoted so much attention and effort would no longer matter—not to him. The result was more than a release of tension; it resembled the indifference, quickly turning into gaiety, he experienced at the beginning of very long airplane trips, for instance to Japan, when he was traveling alone. He would settle down in his space—the travel agent had instructions to put him in the first row of the first-class cabin, with only the bulkhead before him, and the adjoining seat, if possible, blocked and empty. For the next fourteen hours there would be nothing. No intrusions, other than the muffled, whirring noise of the aircraft and meaningless announcements by the crew, no possibility of taking action. Outside, a sky that refused to turn dark. Already during takeoff, he would fall asleep so hard that the steward wouldn't even try to serve him lunch. Later, when he awakened, his feeling of elation bore a whiff of sentimentality, gratitude for everything that had gone well during the past week, and thoughts about Sam, his son. But with his present contentment came no admixture of nostalgia, nothing that was even remotely sentimental. How long could he remain in this state of grace? The tabloids tell you that violent death lurks behind each bush you pass in the Ramble of Central Park, down the street you take circling back to Park Avenue, in the eyes of the kid who wants your money. Death that will take you only after a desperate struggle. For a change, death was face-to-face with a willing victim. Why make the rampage of his disordered cells continue? Why not harvest him now, quietly? Never mind the cancer. That was just a particularly unpleasant detail, a confirmation of what he saw each day as he looked about him and took note of what the once-golden lads and lassies, his contemporaries, were turning into. A shitty decade lay before him, whatever happened. Except for a grandchild, if Sam ever got around to procreating, there was nothing he could anticipate that would be as good as what lay behind.

Since the fall, he had worked even harder than usual. Everywhere, clients wanted to spend less money. Like the agency where he had started, which had seemed so improbably vast in its reach, Mistler, Berry & Lovett too had acquired an airline client, as well as a foreign-car manufacturer. When accounts were put up for review, Mistler was given advance private assurances. Take this as a gesture needed to satisfy the board of directors that every belt-tightening measure has been considered, there is no dissatisfaction with the firm's services. But how could he be sure? He led the presentations to the clients' review committees himself; the accounts stayed with the agency; and ties to the clients seemed as secure as ever. Only the financial ramifications of Peter's forced departure, especially the consequences of the buyback of his shares, had yet to be dealt with, and this Mistler had planned to do as speedily as possible, to prevent fissures developing in the firm, and to trivialize the event. Then, in January, at lunch with Jock Burns, the chairman of Omnium, the only advertising agency other than his own he truly admired, but almost four times larger, Mistler received a veiled, and yet to him clear enough, offer to buy Mistler, Berry. In reply, he put forward a preposterously high multiple of revenues from which, he told Jock, one might derive the price of an agency like his. He heard Jock murmur assent. Trying hard to preserve the sobriety of his mien, he mentioned the vexing problem of client conflicts: other deals had foundered on them. Jock had done his homework. In his opinion, all the difficulties could be managed, and he explained his plan; anyway, he was principally buying the "Mistler element." During the months that followed, with the help of the agency's lawyer, Mike Voorhis, Mistler negotiated the detailed terms of the deal in such secrecy that no one at the agency, except two members of the executive committee, knew of its existence until the weekend before Easter, when he took the entire board of directors to Bermuda, on the pretext of a worldwide strategy review. He had supposed there was a chance that they might disavow him. Nothing of the sort. It had been pleasant, pleasant beyond his expectations, to hear them gasp incredulously, at the opening of the Saturday morning meeting, when he said he was recommending a sale of the firm, and to hear them gasp again, in greater disbelief, when he named the price.

Naturally, the price had to be outrageous, he told them. Why else would I even think of selling?

The next day, at the lunch that concluded their business, they rose to drink his health and sang "For He's a Jolly Good Fellow" twice before he could cut the performance short, with a reminder that the way business conditions were changing it was simply prudent to sell and salt away their money.

Back in New York that evening, after dinner with Clara at their usual neighborhood Italian restaurant, he told her he would like to go to bed right away.

Thank God! She had taken her bath before they went out, and waited in bed, reading, while he soaked in the tub. There was no question in his mind that this was an evening for sex, conducted with a spontaneity that had become infrequent.

But when he reached for her she turned away, and moved his hand to her breast. Not willing to lose the opportunity, he continued to caress her until she pushed him away altogether and said it would be better to go to sleep.

He didn't reply, supposing she had realized how quickly his impulse had passed. But, after a moment, she spoke.

Did you see yourself in the bathroom mirror? You don't just look tired. You look sick. I really mean it. Please don't turn this into one of your jokes. I want you to make an appointment tomorrow morning to see Bill Hurley.

That was the opening gun. After the visit, of necessity, he told her that Hurley had ordered tests but he brushed off her questions about their nature. She had learned long ago that when he was unwilling to speak there was no use insisting. It made him sulk. When the CAT scan and everything else that photography and electronic probes could reveal had finally been read, and both Klein and Hurley said a biopsy was necessary, he looked at his pocket diary and told Hurley it could be on the last Monday in April, because Clara would be away all that week. Otherwise, he wanted it done out of town, for instance in Boston.

I don't wear pajamas when I go to bed with my wife! If she is away she won't be running her hand over bandages and stitches and asking me what happened.

You can't keep this sort of thing from her, said Hurley. It's a serious mistake.

I don't intend to—once I know what this thing is, and what will be done about it, of course I will tell her. I'll also get her to speak to you, and Dr. Steele, and Dr. Klein.

You realize that the wound won't heal within that one week.

Yes, but the bandage will be smaller, and, if I have to, I will tell her a white lie: that I have finally gotten rid of the wart you've been nagging me about. Incidentally, let's ask Dr. Steele to cut that thing off while he's working in the area. Most likely, you will have results of the biopsy by the time she returns.

Well, there was nothing more to wait for; he had just received all the news he or anyone else needed. It was Tuesday. The meeting of the zoological society's board of directors would end on Thursday, so as not to interfere with the weekend. She could be back in New York on Friday, in time for them to go out to Crow Hill together. But he didn't feel ready. It would be better to call as soon as he came home from Anna Williams's dinner and urge Clara to spend the weekend instead with Sam. Why not take advantage of being all the way in San Diego to visit him at Stanford? They might go on one of those wine country drives in Napa. Practically anything had to be better than a weekend of getting acquainted with Mistler's cancer. And it would help when he finally told her if she had an image of an untroubled and recent good time before her—especially one without him in the foreground. This might even be an opportunity, while he was still at the edge of the no-man's-land, before departing on cancer patrol, to give himself a special treat. Something for him to savor in the months or weeks to come. He would need the lingering taste of sweet.

During his last visit to Rick Vernhagen at the hospital, a few days before he died, Vernhagen showed him a small conical object connected to the intravenous feeding tube. It was taped to the bedsheet. He had not noticed it before, because it was covered by Vernhagen's hand. Vernhagen seemed quite impossibly weak. The tube draining globs of dark brown liquid from his stomach, which had been inserted through his nostril and larynx, had frayed his vocal cords. Mistler moved his chair as close as possible to the pillows on which Vernhagen's head rested, and strained to understand him.

You see this, Vernhagen croaked excitedly, moving back and forth the object, which ended in a white plastic button, I love, I love it! You press, like for room service, and it brings nirvana. Yeah, and you don't have to talk with the floor waiter or give him a tip!

The private duty nurse, seeing that Mistler didn't understand, explained that this was a new way of managing pain. When the patient thought it was bad, he squeezed to release morphine. It mixed with the nutrient and immediately flowed into the vein.

You'd be surprised at these guys, she continued. I've never had one use it just to turn on.

Well, he would soon find out how memories of a happy life compared with morphine and Demerol. If Clara asked him to fly out to join her and Sam, he would say that Hurley had ordered him to rest. A long weekend with Clara and Sam wasn't his idea of the treat he needed. They would have time for some of those, perhaps even a vacation, as soon as the semester at Stanford ended, if Sam could manage not to dawdle over year-end examinations and papers and he, Mistler, could complete certain arrangements at the firm and make sure the deal with Omnium was solid. For now, let Pluto grant him, for his piety, a paltry ten days of serene emptiness. He would go to Venice. It was the one place on earth where nothing irritated him. Neither research nor planning was required. He knew where to stay, and which room to ask for, and how to avoid the tourists who feed pigeons at San Marco or follow, like an ugly ship in the wake of the pilot's tug, some garrulous, polyglot person with a funny-colored open umbrella. His conscience need not nag if he failed to look at this or that essential painting or monument. *Vedi Napoli e mori!* It wasn't as though you could capture a masterpiece on your retina and thereby turn it into a funerary object to accompany you, like a pharaoh, to the grave. He had been looking at Venice carefully from the time he was a college boy; whether to see or not to see a particular Titian or Bellini again would be like the choice between saying goodbye to his fellow guests and taking French leave. A nosy and censorious busybody—by definition almost any friend of a married couple—might think it was something of a dirty trick to make this trip without Clara. He knew better. Besides, if she gave signs of resentment, they could return with Sam. He took it for granted that a family vacation, however tiring and difficult, would be indispensable as a matter of ritual, and should take place before he reached the "war zone." Venice would still be there, waiting for mother, father, and son. And perhaps the son's betrothed as well, and her own child. No one should feel excluded.

It was easy to stage-manage his escape. He could leave on Sunday night, before Clara returned from the West Coast— assuming she took his advice and arranged to meet Sam. In fact, if she asked him to join Sam and her for the weekend, the trip to Italy should make his refusal uncontroversial. There was no shortage of pretexts: the Milanese fashion empire he had been courting so assiduously, which had already given the agency work, had asked him, with no notice at all, to a meeting. How could he refuse? As for taking her along, this sort of trip to Milan epitomized everything about his business life she quite rationally hated. Mistler at meetings all day, leaving her stuck with the wife of the client's chairman. Then, in the evening, both of them, like hired performers, having to go through their repertory of small talk about children, odious cultural stereotypes, and the wonders of *funghi porcini* or whatever indigenous equivalent happened to figure at the top of the menu of the pompous restaurant to which they were escorted. She played her part correctly during those occasions. As a general matter she disliked people less than he. But there was no doubt she would gratefully skip Milan if he told her she wasn't specifically expected. The detour to Venice—depending on how and when he mentioned it—why, she would take it either as one more example of his beastly behavior or a welcome obedience to Bill Hurley's orders to slow down.

Mistler was appalled at how efficiently, even as eternity burned his eyes like a desert, he planned the lies he would tell: it was proof that practice makes perfect. While he was at it, might he not also accelerate his liberation from plans and obligations, and call Anna to get out of her dinner? Half past seven. To check on the housekeeper's alertness, he rang instead of using his key. Madame Marie opened at once and reminded him that he was going out and should be getting ready. That was as it should be. How satisfying to have this paragon working for them, a good-looking woman and well trained—not by Clara, of course, who was too egalitarian in her dealings with the staff. They had inherited her from the Belgian consul general departing for an ambassador's post in Sweden. Mistler hoped that Clara would keep the woman and the apartment. In general, it would be easier to leave in the belief that everything else would remain unchanged. Continuity. A video of Mistler's happy life playing on, with Mistler absent. Just like their family photographs: there were hardly any in which he was to be found, for the very good reason that normally he took them. He had just about decided to dial Anna's number when he realized that the exemplary Madame Marie would be disappointed if he broke a long-standing engagement and forced nice Mrs. Williams to rearrange her table and her, Marie, to whip up an unscheduled meal for Monsieur. One mustn't confuse servants, whispered a voice in Mistler's ear, which he recognized as his mother's. Therefore, he thanked Madame Marie, and humming the "Ode to Joy" went upstairs to change.

The West Side. Anna's apartment building faced the Museum of Natural History. Mistler told the driver to be back by ten-thirty. He would make this an early evening.

A huge moon, like a Seville orange cut in half, tender and perplexed, hung over the East Side. He paused to admire it. Vince had paused too, cap in hand, waiting to see Mistler make it safely into the lobby, where the task of protecting him would pass into the hands of whoever had jurisdiction there. A pleasant-looking young man in jeans and white shirt open at the collar stopped beside Mistler, pointed at the sky, and grinned.

Not halfway bad! He spoke with an accent that could be Australian.

Mistler agreed, and told Vince it was really all right to leave. The boy entered the lobby and then the elevator with him, and pressed the button for Anna's floor. Grinning again, he said, We're going to the same place. I'm from New Zealand. Checking out New York. I heard your name when you gave it to the bloke in the lobby. My name is Thomas.

That's my first name too.

Right.

The door of Anna's apartment was ajar. One could hear the braying of the guests. It was a large party after all, probably a buffet; she wouldn't have missed him. Mistler rang the bell and walked in, expecting the boy to follow. But he didn't. Making a circular gesture with his hand, on the fingers of which Mistler noticed several rings, he used a key to let himself into the other door on the landing, which led, presumably, to the bedrooms in the back. A minor mystery. Was this a friend's child ducking in to put on a suit before dinner? A houseboy who was not going to serve at table? Mistler had never met Mr. Williams; he thought he remembered Anna saying years ago that his business consisted of building swimming pools, in Hobe Sound. It had been one of those early and short-blooming marriages that happened to people in the year following their move to New York, like a car crash after college graduation. Without enjoying long tenure, various men had succeeded him as Anna's acknowledged companions. Could this beachcomber be a sex object who had arrived early, and would wait patiently, watching television without sound, until the last guest left, and Anna returned to the bedroom, stretched luxuriously, and kicked off her shoes? Mistler knew the gesture. He would have thought though that Anna was past that sort of after-dinner entertainment.

There was one new face in the living room, the young woman with straight brown hair and no makeup—everybody else was, as Mistler's father might have said, the same as usual only more so. Since Phoebe Gansevoort was nowhere to be seen, either she was Tony Gansevoort's date or Anna had invited her to balance the table. Was it possible that the

Gansevoorts had split without his or Clara's having heard about it? He hadn't seen Tony for a long time. The transformation was unpleasant. His hair, once brown like the young woman's and now dirty gray, was long, possibly longer than hers, and, of all things, gathered in a little ponytail. Before Gansevoort rose to shake his hand, Mistler had a glimpse of his crossed legs and noted that he wore black suede Belgian shoes, the kind that the senior Mr. Mistler called whorehouse slippers, without socks. Doubtless, this was the casual rich chic that had, some years earlier, become prevalent among men of Mistler's age. The costume was completed by an ample, much-too-British blue blazer and tan trousers. What did that old fool mean by dressing on a Tuesday night in New York as though he were at the beach? Mistler couldn't imagine that Phoebe—who had principles about small things—would have let him out of the house got up like someone out of a Tom Wolfe novel. Either she had lost all authority over her husband or there had, in fact, been a revolution in their affairs.

My lady friend, Lina. Have you met? How have you been keeping? Gansevoort's long left arm reached for the woman with brown hair. He pulled her to his side.

I don't think I have.

Mistler wasn't interested in answering the second question. Gansevoort had a penchant for sincerity: saying one was "extremely well" was unlikely to satisfy him. He would want to find out how Mistler really was.

But I know Mr. Mistler. From those photographs of you ballooning in Burgundy. And from your campaign for Love cosmetics! So brilliant! Anna has put me next to you. I am thrilled!

How nice.

Mistler would have preferred to have Anna, or for that matter Phoebe Gansevoort, as his dinner partner. He had known Phoebe forever. There was an I-make-trouble, ready-for-anything, bad-girl quality about her that he liked, the very same quality that had caused him to give her a wide berth, back in the days when she was of an age to attract him. Presumably, he was not placed next to Anna because he was such an old friend. Or was he placed between Anna and this impressionable Lina whose last name he hadn't been told?

The latter turned out to be Anna's plan, but it made no difference. Given the way she had arranged the table, how was he to open himself to an old friend, to speak to her about Clara and Sam, unless he waited for the last guest to leave, and it turned out that the other Thomas wasn't also waiting, for purposes that were Anna's? On her right was one of her authors, Raymond Weiss, a fixture on the Upper West Side, whose most recent work, just published by her, had been greeted by the *New York Times*'s daily reviewer as a catastrophic demonstration of mental confusion and lack of talent, whereas in the *Times Book Review*, a fellow novelist of the same ethnicity and practically the same address, with a new book of her own due out in the fall, solved the problem by using most of the space reserved for her article to deal in general terms with the difficulty of maintaining, over a long career, the excitement of an ambitious, if perhaps excessively inward-turned, oeuvre. Never mind: the judgment of the reading public had just carried Weiss's book to second place on the best-seller list. The party being in fact in Weiss's honor, it was a miraculous piece of luck to see Anna vindicated in the nick of time. Who could blame her for concentrating her attention on the horse that had just run and won? She turned to Mistler occasionally, to

include him in the conversation with Weiss. Mistler understood the signal. He was to say something about the new work,
which he had not read, and its forerunners, equally unknown
to him. Lack of knowledge was not a problem. Anna had
taught him that the last thing an author wishes in such circumstances is to hear a Mr. Mistler express literary opinions in
the nature of criticism, however respectful. To say that he
admired the Master's ability to make characters come alive—
in the new novel and in all the others—was quite enough. He
applied Anna's rule and watched Weiss beam and nod agreement with infinite good nature and lack of modesty. Enough.
Gansevoort was on the other side of the table, to the right,
next to Weiss's agent, an old bag like Weiss except that she
was a woman. Yet Gansevoort seemed to enjoy himself. Good
for him.

So many familiar faces of the living, and there was also
such a surprising crowd of dead people he knew. Father,
Mother, Tante Elisabeth, and, of course, old Sam Abthorp.
They made a family group, together with the grandparents,
although they, having died when he was still at school, didn't
seem to count. Harry Lovett. The confused ghosts of Father's
and Mother's friends, who had mostly died in Florida, with
the greatest discretion, absolving one from the duty of attending their memorial service. Sears, his best friend at school,
killed driving his car into a tree on the way home after the
usual drinks at the golf club. Sears's brother gave him the
news on the telephone. He covered the receiver with his hand
and turned to Clara saying, It's Dick Sears. He has just told me
that George is dead. In a car crash. Naturally, she answered.
Warren, a college classmate and neighbor, whose house he
could see when he looked across Narragansett Bay from the

front lawn at Crow Hill. His death from a heart attack was the most recent. He had been watching his toddler son, the product of a third marriage, play in the sandpile Warren had installed that very weekend, desecrating the one-hundred-and-fifty-year-old lawn. There had to be many more. Perhaps he should check last year's college and school reunion class books. The listing would be somewhere in the back, *In Memoriam*. Didn't Marquand have the late George Apley say he wasn't afraid of dying because he knew so many dead bishops he was sure to get into the best clubs in heaven? It wasn't worth looking up the quotation. To the best of his knowledge, the three prelates among his acquaintances were alive, but the concept had value. He wasn't going as a pioneer; the path was well trodden. He felt that his face had stiffened into a stone monument. He reorganized it into a nice smile.

Mr. Mistler, Mr. Mistler?

That was the friend unto Gansevoort.

You've been lost in a daydream. I hoped to talk to you.

Really? I am very sorry. I was listening to the general conversation. My doctor claims I can hear just fine, but I find it more and more difficult to be sure I follow what is said when more than one person is talking. That must make me look odd—distracted? Concentrating?

How did you come up with the idea, she asked, of ballooning over France to sell California wine? Wasn't that terribly dangerous, putting French wine in the mind of someone to whom you are trying to sell an American Cabernet?

Dangerous? You mean was I at risk of putting my foot in my mouth! The client thought so, just like you. But I believe that French wines are on the consumer's mind anyway, so running away from the problem is no use. The message of the campaign, as I thought of it, was this: Yes, they make excellent wine in France, and they have made it since the time of the Romans, but we have gone over there and learned their secrets. And we have something they don't have—the best and most modern equipment, a scientific approach to the process, and a reliable climate. Remember how each time we cut to the winery in California you see that gorgeous blue sky? Then you see me in my balloon gondola zooming in on a quaint old *chai* and ducking rainstorms. The rainstorms are very important. A message to be conveyed straight to the consumer's unconscious.

It was appalling to talk so much.

But why use yourself in the campaign? Because you are so wildly handsome?

Of course, and also wildly conceited.

Tony never said that about you.

That's proof of his loyalty and discretion.

Then he hasn't told you that I am a home wrecker?

Are you? Of course, I haven't been seeing Tony.

He and his wife have divorced. But it wasn't over me. I am a fairly recent acquisition. I only said I was a home wrecker to see what you would say.

What could I possibly say? Perhaps that Tony's acquisition committee must have stood up and applauded.

As a matter of fact, Mistler thought the old goat had done pretty well. There was a nice warmth about this girl, her skin was clear, and she was right not to cover it with goo. He was willing to bet that she smelled good just the way she was.

It's a busy committee. You know that he has had lots of girls.

I know nothing at all. Tony and I were in grade school

together, and then in college, and I used to run into him and Phoebe at parties like this. That's about all.

Of course, she answered inconsequentially, very nice little boys in those uniform blazers and gray flannel short pants.

Leaving that subject, she told him she was a freelance photographer about to go away, almost immediately, to Europe. A fashion assignment in Milan was a certainty, and her first stop. Later on, there was a story she had been asked to work on about an apartment a Brazilian couple had redecorated in Paris; she was doing that for *Vogue*. It would be nice to have something in between. Did he think his agency might use her? It would be nifty to break in. She grinned. The turn of phrase must have pleased her. He replied that he could ask— if she told him her family name and how he could reach her.

The place card gave only her first name in block letters. She wrote on it with a felt-tip pen she extracted from her pocketbook, "Verano," and underneath a telephone number.

It's in Brooklyn Heights, she told him before he could ask.

What a nice name to have in this season—any season!

I like it too, she replied. I only wish I could get to Italy more often.

Poor thing. Nonsense, there was no reason why she wouldn't. Gansevoort, or his successors, would see to it, if the right assignments didn't come along. His own prospects for frequent travel to Italy were quite a lot dimmer, even though she was probably saying to herself that it must be nice to have Mistler's money and freedom. This unpleasant thought led brusquely to another: the possibility that he had blundered in the Omnium transaction. Really, he had no time for Miss Verano or for thinking how to continue their conversation. He blurted out instead: I am going there too. I will be in Venice, my favorite city, next Monday.

His mistake was thinking that he would go on living like everybody else, and would have a chance to put his money into companies less overvalued than his own agency or Omnium. On that assumption he had insisted that Omnium pay an all-cash price for Mistler, Berry, and had gotten Jock Burns to agree. But this excellent result was all wrong, now that he knew more about himself. If the deal closed before he was dead—he believed it had to, even before his illness showed, since Jock, looking at the agency without Mistler at its head, might want to back out—he would pay tax on the gain on the shares he sold, almost one-third of the purchase price! If he could get Jock to return to his initial offer to pay with Omnium stock instead of cash, the outcome would be far bet-ter. Then there would be no tax on the sale, no estate tax, since he was leaving almost everything to Clara for life, Sam having been taken care of by his family trusts, and best of all, the Omnium shares going into Clara's trust would have a market-value tax basis. Provided they were sold quickly—which he thought they should be, as quickly as could be worked out—there would never be a capital gains tax on the transaction. One thing was clear. He had to speak with Voorhis and Voorhis's tax partner.

All the while Miss Verano talked: colleagues in New York and Europe, the Brooklyn Heights sublet that she might or might not be extending, a cat she could leave with a girlfriend who was pregnant and not accepting work that required travel. He held the respectful pose of an intent listener. A question broke the spell.

May I come to see you in Venice? If you have time. I would like so much to meet your wife too. I have seen pictures of her!

Of course.

In order to put the conversation back on automatic pilot, he added, Tell me what other work you have been doing.

Instead, she observed: So you and Tony aren't close friends. I am sorry about that.

Then Anna stood up, and Mistler quickly moved to the living room. Gansevoort came up to him.

How do you like her? You were a fan of Phoebe's, weren't you?

You mean do I like Lina? Charming girl. I was glad to meet her and to see you. Look, I'm going to kiss Anna and sneak out. I've got to call some people before their bedtime.

On his way out, he said goodbye also to Lina.

Thank you, she whispered. Don't forget Venice.

[II]

PUSHING HIS LUGGAGE CART along the airport building to the jetty, where water taxis dock, he began to feel light-headed, as though he had been puffing too long on a cigar that bled. Had he begun to resemble his mother and certain old ladies of her acquaintance, always on the lookout, like border police, for twinges of pain, swellings, and eruptions of the skin not identified before? Otherwise, why was it so urgent to know whether this mixture of fatigue and nausea was a gen-uinely new feature in the landscape of his existence? Since the conversations with the doctors, he had begun to wish for an hourglass that would show, moment by moment, the ebbing of his strength. Probably, no instrument existed sensitive enough to distinguish the effect of a night on the plane, and the wait at Roissy for the connection, from the goings-on in that deviant and numb organ inside him, but at least some of the feeling that he was unable to take another step had to be a message it was sending. Mistler steadied himself against the railing, closed his eyes, then opened them to stare at the water. The luggage cart was no friend. Had he called for a porter he might have leaned on his arm, however indelicate the gesture. Taking a deep breath, to clean his mouth, lungs, and brain, he asked the dispatcher to get him a taxi.

A light mist clung to the surface of the lagoon. Mistler stood in the aft, incurious and excited, waiting for the islands to appear. The spray cooled his face. He lit a cigar to cover the taste of his saliva and quickly threw it away. Had Clara been with him, he might have held her hand. She always had chewing gum or mints in her handbag. Would it have been better to bring her? This trip, the white lie he had told, the longing to find something he couldn't quite define, were they some sort of bet? In that case, he was on both sides of it. What could he expect from any action? In a few weeks or months, when the greater unpleasantness began, he would see this holiday for what it was—an expensive farce paid for in unfamiliar units of strength that no amount of rest or sleep could renew. Was it then that he would finally learn it was no use always sailing so close to the wind, determined to stay on course, obsessed by the effort? They entered the channel. The boatman opened the throttle, leaving a wake like a fan of white feathers. Here and there, solitary dinghies swayed on anchor. Men fishing for eel? The sun was in Mistler's eyes. He put on his dark glasses, and, as though the gesture had magic properties, the tower of Madonna dell'Orto, the Fondamente Nuove, became visible, gathered volume. San Michele was before them. The boat slowed down. Mistler recognized successively the shapes of Santa Maria della Misericordia and the Gesuiti, the entrance to the Arsenal. He would have liked to stop the boat altogether, to have the shoreline remain in place for a moment, to take in the city more strongly. But it required too great an effort to go forward through the cabin to speak to the boatman and deal with his bewilderment at a request not included in the fare. He settled for looking hard. Facades of palaces appeared mysteriously and disappeared as the boat threaded its way through the lateral canals. They passed the Hotel Metropole. San Giorgio was before them, dead ahead. As they turned toward the mouth of the Grand Canal, the Dogana and the Salute appeared. Shimmering of blue, gold, and white. The boat went into reverse, a man who had spent his life doing just that caught the line the boatman threw him and made it fast. For the first time in his life feeling something that might be seasickness, Mistler stepped ashore and entered the lobby of the hotel.

Signor Anselmo, the chief concierge, and his assistant, both of whom Mistler considered, depending on his mood, either friends or a species of questionable investments, rather like tax shelters that returned no income but made unending calls for cash, came forward, in their haste upstaging the assistant manager.

La signora is already here, murmured Signor Anselmo.

Was the man mad? Did he not recognize him? What was he mumbling about? Clara had called just before he left for the airport, saying she was in San Francisco. If this were some sort of a 1940s movie stunt, she might, of course, in reality have been telephoning from Kennedy and taken an Alitalia plane to Milan, in which case she would have beaten his own flight via Paris and gotten to Venice first. He had never known her to like flashy surprises or practical jokes. As practical jokes went, this one, however well intentioned, would be unwelcome; infuriating wouldn't be too strong. He didn't have enough time to be patient, let alone amused, by people's crossing his plans. Of course, she didn't know that.

La signora brought flowers and left her luggage downstairs. Shall I have it taken up?

Certainly, with my bags. I need them right away.

Welcome to your home in Venice, Mr. Mistler. You have your usual apartment. That was the assistant manager.

Thank you. Then there is no need to accompany me. I'll just take the key.

La signora took it.

Then please give me the double.

He waved away the hand that would have relieved him of his briefcase. His address book was inside it. Very early morning in New York, perfect time to catch people at home, some of them before they got out of bed. No matter how he felt, this was the time for his telephone calls. The elevator stopped at the second floor. He followed the blood-red carpet to the double door at the end of the corridor, and opened it. A raincoat hung in the little foyer. Not Clara's. The two enormous windows of the sitting room that gave on the canal were open; "I've Got You Under My Skin," whistled with weird accuracy, could be heard from the other room, which was on the right. The door was ajar. Clara didn't whistle; she sang her Cole Porter repertory off-key. Mistler put his briefcase on the sofa, knocked, and, without waiting for an answer, walked in. It was, after all, his suite. On the bed, wearing a white terry-cloth peignoir marked with the hotel's insignia, sat Lina Verano. She was drying her toes, one by one, with a small hand towel.

Mr. Mistler! She stood up. Her hair was wet, and hung in strands on her perfectly smooth cheeks. She was prettier than he had found her at Anna's, but in the strong daylight seemed less juvenile.

Please excuse me. Your plane must have been early. I didn't think you would be here for another hour, so I took a bath. I would have put everything back so you wouldn't have ever noticed. Look, I brought you all of these.

She pointed. There were roses and peonies—white, red, and pink—on the dressing table in the bedroom and on the coffee table and marble-topped gueridons in the sitting room.

Aren't they beautiful? Say something, Mr. Mistler!

Only one thing comes to mind: What are you doing in my hotel room?

Someone, presumably the porter, was pounding on the outside door. Mistler shouted, *Avanti!* His luggage. A moment later, the porter reappeared, pulling behind him a gray suitcase on wheels like a mutt on a leash. Mistler tipped him, and waited while the man disposed of the stuff in the bedroom.

I repeat, what are you doing here?

You knew I was coming to see you in Venice. You said it was all right. I couldn't find a room in any of the *pensioni* I know, so I came here, just to meet you. I left my suitcase downstairs. I am sorry I used your bathroom. I guess I didn't read you as well as I thought. I sort of thought you might be glad to see me. Amused. Who knows?

And what was my wife going to say?

I knew she wasn't coming! I called the hotel the day after Mrs. Williams's party to make sure you were staying here, and they said the reservation was for you alone. Then, to make sure, I also checked the airline. Do you mind so very much? I can leave right away. If I find a place to stay, I'll call you tomorrow. I may have to try a hotel in Mestre. They're less expensive.

Good Lord, said Mistler. You can't walk out of here dressed like this. They'd take the peignoir from you at the front desk, and I hate to think of the riot that would follow. Look, give me fifteen minutes. I'm very tired and I have some telephone calls to make.

I am so sorry. I can stay in the bedroom while you telephone.

She knelt down beside the dreadful suitcase, took a book from it, and told him she wouldn't mind if he closed the door.

He had seen Voorhis the day after Anna Williams's dinner. Right away he told Mistler that he was not mistaken about the tax, and then asked what was he worrying about, it had been such a coup to get Omnium to agree to pay cash, how could the change to a stock deal be explained to the board or to employee shareholders who weren't on the board? Wasn't cash the better deal?

That's what I thought too, said Mistler, but I don't anymore. I have changed my mind. If we do a stock deal, anyone who doesn't like Omnium stock can sell, and those who believe in owning advertising agency shares can hold and pay no tax.

There are restrictions on selling, that's why we didn't like the stock deal in the first place.

Get rid of as many of them as you can. When they think of it, they will see that, in reality, restrictions aren't that important. They should concentrate on the transaction going through. Don't forget they can't sell shares in Mistler, Berry at all. I think I can tell the employees that swapping Mistler, Berry shares for Omnium is in itself a real diversification. They will have an investment in the Mistler, Berry component, which it's up to them to make grow, and also in all the other agencies and businesses Omnium owns, that others are running, that have different clients and so on, and that will be salable, even if there are restrictions. Besides, I think I can get Jock Burns to pay a higher price if I say we will take his shares instead of cash.

It wasn't hard to guess that if Mistler revealed why he had changed his mind Voorhis would pounce on the question of whether the reason had to be disclosed. As a matter of school-boy honor, Mistler knew it should be. School days were over. So far as he, Mistler, was concerned, it was out of the question to tell Jock a lie face-to-face or in the contract, but no one had asked about his health or that of anybody on his executive committee. All that Omnium's lawyers and investment bankers seemed to care about was key man insurance. Did they have it? Was Mistler insured? Who else? Yes, and for greater amounts than Omnium had thought. The insurance policies were produced for inspection. They would get their money for one key man sooner than they had hoped. It amused Mistler to think how he had always hated paying for insurance. In fact, the firm also carried term insurance on his life—ten million dollars, if his recollection was right—payable to his estate. Perhaps that wasn't important in the grand design of his exit, but he couldn't help thinking it made a nice going-away present.

Does Omnium have enough authorized shares to do the deal with stock, he asked Voorhis, and do they have to go to shareholders for approval?

He waited impatiently while Voorhis searched on his insufferably messy desk for Omnium's financials and his calculator. After what seemed to be a series of mistakes, he said, I have it. Yes. At yesterday's bid price, more than enough. By how much do you think you can get them to up the price?

Maybe fifteen percent.

Still enough, and it doesn't have to be approved.

They can do it without a shareholders' meeting, solicitation of proxies, and all that stuff?

Yes, they aren't on the New York Stock Exchange. I'll double-check, but I am quite sure it's all right.

That was a relief, like a car starting when you fear the battery might be dead, the cork not crumbling as you draw it out of a bottle of old wine, an ejaculation heroically postponed at the last moment. He wanted the deal done, done fast. Voorhis had told him that Omnium's due diligence was finished and the agreements were almost in final form.

How about our own due diligence? Voorhis asked. We haven't done any to speak of, since they were paying cash, but if we are taking shares, shouldn't we do an investigation of the company?

No, replied Mistler. We'll rely on their SEC filings, and make them guarantee them and anything additional you think we must have. Please get this show on the road. By the way, what are we guaranteeing? Have you agreed to anything unusual? What do we say about adverse developments in our business?

They have asked for all sorts of things, but now it's come out just as you said you wanted it: we warrant our financials and that we haven't been told by major clients that they want to put their accounts up for review. And we only warrant as of the day we sign the sale agreement. After that, the deal is as good as closed.

Keep it that way.

That's right, thought Mistler, stick to your job and leave the unpleasant questions to me. Such as: Why am I doing this? The cash deal is a fine deal. Clara and Sam are rich anyway, and Sam won't know what to do with all that money. It's one thing to remain silent and let the deal go forward. Even that isn't quite right. But to renegotiate with Burns, as though everything were all right! What's the point of stepping over the line that separates you from men whose hands you wouldn't shake? The answer is, I have always finished everything I have begun, I have always had my way. Come to think of it, putting Peter Berry out to pasture wasn't a nice thing to do either. The deal was good for Mistler, Berry before I knew I was sick, and it's still good. Maybe better, because good old Jock Burns will keep the agency together, whereas I have no successor capable of doing that. What kind of deal this is for Omnium, that's his business. Will my father turn over in his grave? I'll ask when I see him. But if he is doing any rotating, it should be on account of what he did to his own firm!

He saw that Voorhis was staring at him.

Thomas, just what is the problem?

There is nothing the matter with the agency, nothing at all.

The trouble was that he really liked Voorhis a lot. Otherwise, he would have forgone hearing the opinion of this square and very honest man, so in love with his watercolorist wife, and so unconscious of the advances she made to his principal client. All carefully ignored by that client, of course.

Look, old friend, he said, there is a personal problem. I am dying. But I think I can make it in reasonable shape through the closing, and probably for a decent while afterward, if you really move this transaction along. All right? How much risk do we have?

He stopped Voorhis's wail in midsentence.

We'll leave that sort of thing for another time. Right now, only my doctors and you know, and I'll keep it that way as long as necessary. And don't you tell anybody, not even your wife!

When did you find out?

For sure? Only yesterday. Back to business now. How much legal risk am I taking?

I want to think.

Voorhis wiped his eyes. If the deal closes, he said, very little—I mean Omnium might be able to argue that in these circumstances the nondisclosure of your illness was a fraud, and try to unscramble the deal, but I doubt they would do it. It wouldn't be good for Omnium to take the position that one man mattered that much, and they hadn't asked any questions. They would end up looking stupid to clients and financial analysts. For the same reasons, I don't think they would go after your estate for damages. Anyway, damages would be hard to prove. If they find out before the closing, though, they may try to walk. Do you want to know what I think as a matter of business ethics?

Probably not. But tell me anyway.

It's not good. You shouldn't do it. To those who will eventually put two and two together—many will—asking for shares at this time will make you look sharp and selfish. There is a more important question: Have you put one over on Jock Burns, even if you leave the transaction as it is? Either way, your memory will be tarnished.

I get your point. Have I ducked any of their questions?

None that I know of. Nothing they have come out and asked.

Have you ducked any on my behalf? I don't see how you could have. You didn't know anything.

That's true. But this is so important, I think it would be right to disclose even if they weren't smart enough to ask.

Good. Now I will tell you something: The "Mistler element" Jock Burns is so keen on, if there is such a thing at all, is in the agency now, not in me. The boys and girls I have trained can do it all. Some clients will miss me, but they are with us for the product, not my personal charm.

You don't believe that.

I do, and not only for the sake of this argument. Just think of my age. Under the employment agreement you got me to sign, I can retire and become a consultant to them at sixty-five, or I can retire and do nothing. I would never be a consultant. I don't need the money. It follows that if I am not run over by a taxi, and don't die of cancer, as I am doing, the longest they can have me for is about three and a half years. Balls!

In Voorhis's presence, from his office, he called Jock and said, Look, I must tell you I have changed my mind.

He thought he could hear the dismay on the other end of the line.

No, not about doing the deal with you, I wouldn't do that once we have shaken hands, but I now think I was wrong to ask for cash. We'll take Omnium shares, but in exchange I need some improvement in the price.

Immense relief. That too was audible. There is hardly a need for those video telephones we are always threatened with.

That could be tricky. How much?

I will tell you by the end of the week. That will give you the weekend to think it over, because, after we have spoken, I will leave for a week—I'll be in Venice. I will call you for the answer as soon as I get to my hotel there. Please tell your colleagues that I am making a very serious request. I don't change my mind often.

Now that he was in Venice, that call to Jock had to be made

at once. If he said no, Mistler had decided not to put up a fight. He would take it as a sign from heaven and the sensitive senior Mr. Mistler to leave well enough alone. But if he said yes, the tax savings would be there, and the fifteen percent increase in price would be a nice protective cushion in case his departure hurt the stock—but it wouldn't hurt Omnium's stock that much, not nearly, anyway not for very long if the market remained generally strong. He dialed Jock's number in Short Hills.

Here I am, he said, in my Venetian corner suite, surrounded by flowers, ready to go out to eat cannelloni as soon as we have finished our conversation, and feeling unpleasantly guilty about this wake-up call. Have you worked your way through the numbers?

It's all right. Go eat your cannelloni and send me a bill for the wine. Love to Clara. You've got a deal. Everybody here is happy about this vote of confidence in Omnium. Now look, Thomas: have a good vacation. You've been looking pretty green about the gills.

Mistler had made the call standing up, leaning against the couch. He sat down and called his own secretary.

Hold my faxes until this evening, he told her. I am not up to them today. And please call Mr. Voorhis as soon as you get to the office. Make sure you get through to him. Or you can call him at home now. The message is that Jock Burns has said yes. Yes, I said yes. No change from what I have proposed most recently. Voorhis will know what I mean.

He opened the door to the bedroom. Of course, the girl was still there, in a chair by the window, reading. How would she have gotten out?

You have finished, she said. I didn't want to disturb you.

Now I had better go. This was a terrible mistake. I hope you can forgive me. My things are in the bathroom. It will take me just a minute.

Her diction was like a polite child's. Brought up strictly by lower-middle-class parents. Salt of the earth.

Look here, he said, let's not make a mountain out of a molehill. I am tired from the trip and I need a bath. But I've just pulled off quite a stunt in my business, and it will give me pleasure to take you to lunch. After my bath. We'll talk over lunch. Although, actually, I want a cup of coffee first. Would you like one too?

There was something humble or submissive about the way she nodded her head that he immediately regretted. He rang for room service. It didn't seem to him that he had treated her badly. After all, he hadn't invited her to show up in his hotel room with her flowers and her suitcase, he hadn't flirted with her at dinner, and for all she knew if he wasn't going to Venice with Clara it was to meet someone else. What gave her the right to expect him to make a pass, to jump her, as his father would have put it? Was that some sort of tribute she was due? And what about his loyalty to Gansevoort? It was a fact that he couldn't care less about Gansevoort. Being no dope, she had probably figured that out.

The coffee was very hot. He drank a second cup and lit a cigarette. It really was time to take that bath. After the bath, he would call the chambermaid, and ask her to unpack for him. It didn't matter if she made a mess. He would straighten the stuff out after the nap.

Could I have some more coffee too?

He had forgotten her. I am sorry, he said, really very sorry. You see, it's quite true that I am tired. I won't be long in my bath. Then we will get some fresh air. Would it be all right if I banished you to there? He pointed in the direction of the other room.

Her clothes were folded in a neat pile on the taboret at the head of the bathtub. Right next to it, on the floor, was her camera bag. He moved it all to the bedroom. When he had finished dressing, he found her in a chair at the window, the book in her hand. She had not changed out of the bathrobe.

You are a serious reader. As soon as you are ready, we can go out and find something delicious to eat. I know just where I might take you.

Could we have lunch here instead? It's such a beautiful room. I'd like to stay quietly in this chair.

Certainly. One of those enormous books with a menu in it must be in the desk. Here, see if you can find anything you like.

Cannelloni, she said. The crab cannelloni.

How extraordinary! I have just told a man over the telephone that I was going out to a restaurant to eat cannelloni, but I only said it for rhetorical effect. Now I'll really have them. Do you mind if we have red wine? We'll have a good one—*un vino stupendo!* That nice man said I could send him the bill for the wine.

She didn't mind red wine. As she shook her head, she looked up. He saw that she had been crying.

It's all right now, she said. Right after lunch, I'll get dressed and leave.

An idyll in the making spoiled. Not the first one. As soon as she asked to have lunch in the room, he thought of the first visit he and Clara had made to this hotel. It was early summer. She was pregnant with Sam. The trip was then a more tiring affair. They had taken the day plane from New York to Paris. Her ankles were badly swollen by the time they landed, so he decided they should not go on to Venice the next evening. Instead, they spent another night in Paris, and took the night train to Venice the following day. They might have had this very apartment; that was the sort of thing Clara could have told him at once. Her ankles hadn't gotten any better, and her face looked startled and flushed. They telephoned the obstetrician. Presumably because she was going to talk about bladder functions, she asked Mistler to go into the bedroom. Her voice carried, and although he had been careful not to eavesdrop, he realized when she was about to say goodbye. He knocked, opened the door, and asked whether he could have just one word with Dr. Wills, chosen by Clara because he was the New York pope of the natural birth method, although he was attached to Lenox Hill and not the hospital where Bill Hurley's uncle was on the staff.

Hello, hello, he shouted across the bad connection. I just wondered if you could quickly tell me what's happening. I would very much like to understand.

Dr. Wills cut him short. It's all been explained to your wife. Just do what she says, Mr. Mistler.

Bang. The receiver went down.

What did he tell you?

Silence. Like this girl, she had sat down at the window, and started crying. Great big tears ran down both sides of her nose, which was the part of her face he liked best because it turned up like an unanswered question, and a drop of mucus hung from her left nostril. Her chin was quivering, and so were her lips, which had the shape of delicate peeled shrimps, normally another part of her he liked. Now they were dry to the point of cracking. She was accustomed to using a very pale Guerlain lipstick—there was no way to talk her into switching, although he had just completed his first campaign for Love cosmetics, and she knew that he considered himself honor-bound to buy his clients' products—but she had apparently forgotten to reapply it before she stepped out of the gondola at the hotel landing, if indeed she had put on any that morning. A heap of misery and self-pity. She was so big boned that the pregnancy hardly showed, and he thought that she could get away with regular clothes for at least another month, but she wore a periwinkle-blue maternity dress with a wide black patent-leather belt that made her stomach stick out more than in any other garment. The flat thong sandals had been made for her by a cobbler on Hydra the previous summer. Her toes were swollen to a darker blue than the dress. The varnish on her toenails had peeled. Really, there was no need for such neglect; it wasn't as though she lacked money for her beloved Elizabeth Arden. And those wretched ankles! The skin was very tight and mottled. He knelt down beside her and touched it. When he took his finger away, it left a white depression. Unable to remember when he had last seen her handbag, he stole a glance around the room. There it was, on the armchair next to the other window. Red box calf. He had bought it at Gucci's, in New York. Did that huge valise contain two items of clothing that could conceivably match? He had staggered under the weight, hoisting it onto the overhead luggage rack, the smelly and unpleasant porter having abandoned them at the door of their compartment.

He repeated his question. For heaven's sake, Clara, what did that man tell you?

She sniffed. Nothing. He said I should get all the rest I can. And you should lay off badgering me. Including at night.

Last time that subject came up, he said we could, after the third month.

That was in New York. Now that you've dragged me here, when all I wanted to do was stay in the country, I can't.

All right, he said. It's past one o'clock. Why don't you wash your face—or take a bath if you feel hot—and we'll go out to lunch. Afterward, you can get some sleep. You will soon feel a whole lot better.

Let's order some food here.

She studied the menu. It took forever.

I want cannelloni. Ask if they have meat cannelloni. Starting this evening, I'll have nothing except fish.

The waiter wheeled in the table. The mineral water, red wine in a carafe, cold sliced veal for Mistler. Under the silver bell, those cannelloni. When the waiter lifted the cover, the smell overpowered Mistler, as though it were he who was pregnant. He drank a glass of water, then all the wine, watching her eat, unable to touch his veal. She was a slow eater. The man returned as soon as Mistler rang—he might have been lurking outside the door—and brought dessert. Wild strawberries were in season. He asked for more wine, disregarding the face she made, and drank it with the coffee.

I'll take that nap, she said. Do you think you can stay out of the bedroom? You could visit a church or something.

He didn't bother to point out that the Accademia was already closed for the day and churches wouldn't reopen until five. On the ground floor of the hotel he found a toilet. The sun was unpleasantly strong. He regretted having left his dark glasses on the living room desk. The café orchestra on the shaded side of the Piazza San Marco was sawing its way through "Besame Mucho." He strolled toward it, and identified the woman at once. She was drinking something green. The adjacent table was free. No risk. If he caught the clap, it would have time to declare itself before he next slept with Clara. The woman's apartment—a room, really, with the toilet, portable bidet, and washstand curtained off—was nicely convenient, on his way back to the hotel, across the bridge from the black face of San Moisè. She had the knack of turning herself into a ball, her knees as high as her face. After the first time, he asked if he could stay for the rest of the afternoon. I have no *appuntamenti*, she told him. Great! It was as good a place for a rest as any.

Why had he married Clara? There was no reason he shouldn't have. That was the answer to which he usually returned. They met at Sunday lunch in Greenwich, at Harry Lovett's place, and, when the meal was over, he offered to drive her back to New York. She had come out on the train, on Friday. It seemed that her father, who taught history at Wesleyan, was a cousin of Harry's wife. In the car she let him touch her on the thigh under her skirt, and, after dinner at Rao's—where she had never been—came back to his apartment. Oh, she wasn't at all that kind of girl. That was quite clear, but she didn't make a point of explaining. Nor did she tell him beforehand that she was a virgin. That, in his view, was exceptionally gallant. Her looks were terrific, so American squeaky clean that the same week he arranged to have her photographed for a series of contour-sheet ads. The first one, full page, in color strong enough to bowl you over, ran on the inside cover of the *Times Sunday Magazine* Labor Day issue, and made her colleagues at the development office of the Museum of Modern Art drool with envy. Mistler's father had died during the previous autumn. Horror! A memory that couldn't be borne. His mother was hesitating between staying in New York, in the Sutton Place apartment that was really too big, and moving to the Palm Beach house, with some sort of pied-à-terre in town to be acquired later. The only son and the father's secretary, with the son's secretary pitching in, barely sufficed to keep up with Mrs. Mistler's affairs, which seemed to grow daily in complexity and strangeness. He waited for the other shoe to drop. When was Mother going to say to Thomas darling how she had thought it over, even talked about it to that adorable Jane Hollander, and decided that it would be easy to create very elegant and comfortable bachelor quarters for him at Sutton Place. Something like a flat in the Albany! A big sigh might follow: Your father would have been pleased! Then Thomas could move out of that dingy, eccentric flat in Gramercy Park. Really, what other man of his means, and with his new situation in business to uphold, would live deliberately like a bohemian? The cook has so much time on her hands, and Pedro too! They would love to keep darling Thomas's brogues polished, pass the martinis, and whip up the *sauté de veau* for his dinner parties. One could see New Jerusalem rising from widowhood and trusts. What better way was there to fend all this off than to marry Clara Robinson? Robinson was a good Hartford name. In principle, not even Mrs. Mistler could object, even though these particular Robinsons had no money. With a sigh for what might have been, she moved to Palm Beach and offered them as a present the Sutton Place apartment, full of sun and river air, barges and tugboats drifting across the windows. But Clara foolishly refused it, preferring the "unique baronial duplex home" on Park Avenue that a gentlewoman turned real estate broker, the hard-up mother of one of her college roommates, showed her. Jane Hollander never got to do the pied-à-terre, which would have been a swell assignment. And, within eighteen months, the old lady was also dead, unmourned.

Actually, I am quite stupid about Italian wines, Mistler confided to the girl as the waiter wheeled in their lunch, so I use the price method of shopping. This is the most expensive Piedmont red on the wine list. It should be all right.

As she didn't reply, he waited for the man to open the wine and said, Pour it into the lady's glass. She will taste.

It's very good.

Thank God for that. Let's eat our lunch. I don't know about you, but I'm starved.

Please, Mr. Mistler. May I say something?

Come, come. You could really call me Thomas.

All right, I'll try to remember. How can I make you believe this? I wanted to see you in Venice as soon as you said you would be here. I would like to photograph you. I didn't tell you that, because I thought you would say no. Probably people ask you all the time. I was sure you would say no if I asked you to do it in New York, because you are so busy. I also thought that if you liked what I did, you would really help me get work from your agency. I wasn't going to throw myself at you.

She began to sob. Mistler detested other people's lies. He also hated women's tears, and the noise women make when they cry. Therefore, trying to sound fierce, he told her, Stop that at once or there won't be any photo sessions now or ever!

It worked. She actually smiled.

You see, I guessed you would stay at this hotel. So I called up and asked when Mr. and Mrs. Mistler were expected, and right away the receptionist told me that you were arriving today—and alone. It was very cheeky to ask to be shown to your room, but I wanted to clean up and had nowhere else to go.

It seemed needlessly cruel to tell her that there are showers for day-trippers and facilities for checking one's gear near the main post office, so Mistler held his tongue.

Could we pretend that this never happened? Would you give me another chance?

The two glasses of heavy wine he had drunk had made themselves felt. It didn't matter whether or how badly the girl lied. She was sitting across the table from him in his hotel room, presumably naked under that peignoir. If this were all about photography, wouldn't she have gotten dressed? The coarseness of the insight excited him. The smallest sign from him should suffice. After all, this was a girl who slept with Gansevoort.

Don't worry so much, he told her. It's not necessary to talk about giving you a second chance. I was very tired, and under some pressure because of business when I walked in. Now I feel better, and it was certainly nice not to have lunch alone. Let's be friends—I thought we almost were when I left that dinner at Anna's.

Thank you.

In two steps she was at his side, had put her arms around his neck, and kissed him on the cheek. He had guessed right. There was nothing under the terry cloth.

He patted her on the back, told her it was all right, and pointed in the direction of the chair she had left. Really, he thought, I mustn't rush this, one way or the other, I am in no state to know what I want. He offered her a cigarette. She didn't smoke, she informed him, but didn't mind if others did, she even liked it.

What about Gansevoort, he asked her. Hasn't he retired from that law firm? In his place, I would have come to Italy with you.

He wanted to, but I didn't.

Why is that?

I don't think it's good for me to be involved with old men. It's like getting into a rut. I want to get married, but I don't want to end up being someone's nurse.

At once she covered her mouth, and looked so embarrassed that he laughed.

You're right, that's a big problem. You are willing to be with Tony a good deal, but not too much, and you don't want to be too serious because that might interfere with finding someone young and nice.

She nodded her head.

And how does old man Tony feel about that? If you don't mind telling me.

He doesn't like it. He gets quite moody. I think he complains to Phoebe—I mean Mrs. Gansevoort. They're still friends.

As soon as she said that, she giggled. No, she couldn't be more than twenty-five; perhaps a very young looking twenty-eight.

There was a little wine left in the bottle. He poured it into his glass, hers being full, and emptied it.

Drink mine too, she said. I think I've had quite enough.

So had Mistler. He had forgotten to ask to have his clothes put away. The weight pressing on his shoulders was becoming heavier. He was a slave in a gabardine suit, bent over, crouching, supporting a palace balcony until the end of time or the building's final ruin.

I have to have that nap, he said. What are we going to do about you? Shall I ask whether they have a room in this hotel? Or at the Monaco? They know me, that might help.

These hotels are much too expensive. I'll take another walk—and see about a *pensione*. In Italy, sometimes there is no room if you telephone, but if you show up in person it's different.

Leave the suitcase, if you like, and keep the key they gave you. When you come back, if the door to the bedroom is closed that means I am still asleep. But I doubt I will sleep very long. Don't disappear completely. Now that we are friends, we might have dinner together—at a restaurant.

This was a familiar misery: broken, to the point of obsession, by the need to sleep, and knowing that unconsciousness would remain just beyond the reach of his fingertips, that a succubus would deny him rest, tormenting his skin with itches in one unpredictable place after another, as though it were playing hide-and-seek with him. He closed the shutters in the bedroom but didn't draw the curtains, thinking the strips of light that remained visible would save him from the mistake of trying to force sleep by the power of complete darkness. The brocade bedcover was voluminous and stiff. Where was he to store it? He didn't want to disturb the stately harmony of the room by throwing it on the floor, making of it a mound of crumpled red and gold. It would be best to ring for the chambermaid and ask her to open the bed, but, during the hours that followed lunch, the staff was hard to find. If he got tired of waiting, he would have to take steps to make sure the woman didn't appear. That would mean running the risk of being misunderstood. The chambermaid—perhaps the chambermaid and her assistant!—would disregard the "Do Not Disturb" sign, rush into the room, huffing and puffing, followed by their faint smell, just as he had managed to doze off. It wasn't worth it. He put on his pajamas, got a sweater to cover his bare feet, for reassurance not warmth, and lay down on top of the fully made bed. Hopeless! He got a glass of water and a sleeping pill and had swallowed it moments before he remembered Clara. That call couldn't be postponed, too bad about the sedative. It would be early afternoon in New York before he awakened; he had promised to call in the morning. All that time she would have been waiting. Indeed, she answered at once, and he fought back as best he could.

How could you think it? I had a late lunch, then I started getting ready for a nap, you know how long that takes when I'm all wound up, I haven't even read the paper today, and I am almost ready to go to sleep. Tonight? I don't know, it depends on when I wake up and how I feel. No, nothing planned. Embargo on plans. Yes, I am already in Venice. That was a change of plans. Really, very handsome gesture, they came here and we met all morning. It went well, the snake oil still sells. No, they're on their way back to Milan, we've got the whole account except for some work I didn't want, so I am beginning my rest-and-risotto cure. No, I don't mind if you don't take the next plane over, in fact I beg you not to do it. I'm not the best company, not even for myself. You were right, I need the rest and time to think about some stuff. No, not a delayed midlife crisis—mostly office. Oh, Sam brought the girl? How nice. Of course, it was nice of him, what makes you think he brought her because he didn't want to be alone with you? He's a grown man, if he hadn't wanted to be with you he would have said so or invented something he had to do elsewhere. It's a sign of confidence in you and in her and I am thrilled. But it went badly? Not completely? That's good. Sunday night? That's right, I couldn't reach you because I was in the air. And what happened? Clara dear, you were tired from the week in San Diego, and all the driving around, none of this is particularly startling. Probably you were hungry too. Yes, they are intolerant. Sam shouldn't have spoken to you that way, not in front of the girl, or even afterward. Will I talk to him? Yes, perhaps this very evening. I agree that Monique isn't just what you and I might have imagined as a daughter-in-law, but it's not up to us. Why do you think we won't have grandchildren? I think that her having that one child already will make her want to have another one with Sam. Sure, and being a stepfather will make Sam used to the idea of children. I would love to see Sam have a baby, you can't imagine how very much. Tomorrow. I will call you tomorrow, before you go to that dinner. Anna Williams's party? Except for Anna and a photographer woman Tony Gansevoort brought, it was like a party at Dracula's castle. By the way, did you know they had split up? Oh yes? No, you never told me. The usual dinner, dressed-up fancy corpses pretending to be people I've known all my life. Disconcerting to realize they doubtless had the same impression of me. No you don't look like an old witch. You are a young witch. "I don't love you, dear, I worship you!" These last words Mistler sang into the telephone.

The sleeping pill had turned into Benzedrine. Mistler thought that if anyone dared him he could do the two-hundred-meter dash. Instead he dialed Sam's number. Surprise and tenderness: instead of the voice mail of the Stanford English department, he got his only son.

Have you heard? Mom and I had a blowout. She drank most of the bottle of Chardonnay I ordered before the waitress brought the appetizers, and started working on Monique. In fact, she had gotten going on her first thing on Saturday, as soon as we left for the drive. It was a classic Mom overture: Do you think you are really up to driving Sam's car? It's so powerful! After that she made those I-am-going-to-die faces every time Monique got out of her lane to pass, all of which Monique saw in the rearview mirror. The temperature dropped to ten below zero!

Ouch! Why didn't you drive yourself? You know she gets scared.

I thought that way I could turn around and talk to Mom without her telling me to keep my eyes on the road, and also point out stuff to her as we went by. Besides, Monique loves to drive. I'd give her the BMW, but it seems like making a big statement. She might not like that. All right, it was a mistake. And then, can you imagine it, she didn't say one word to Linda or about her. Really! A four-year-old kid sitting next to you in the backseat of the car, and you pretend she isn't there?

That's not too good. But I think it had to do with that car of yours doing what—sixty? sixty-five?—on winding roads.

All right, I said that was a mistake. But then at dinner it was really awful. She got into this monologue about how all the new family therapies are fascistic, and the only true way is through Freud, and every time Monique tried to put a word in about how not all family therapies are the same, for instance how in her practice she is really very nondirective, Mom just rolled on like a tank.

And how are things between you and Monique? That's

more important. I think Monique is a very grown-up lady, and she'll get over the dinner with Mom.

They're fine, Dad, just fine. We're still going to get married at Christmas.

That's good news. Congratulations! If I were you, I would call Mom and be nice to her. I think she is sorry the visit didn't work out better. You know that I am in Venice until the end of the week. That gives her a lot of time to brood. There is one other thing. Do you think you can get your work done by the beginning of June, so that I could invite you for a short family vacation? We might spend a couple of weeks in the country, but I prefer getting away. How do you feel about Venice? I like it so much here I wouldn't mind coming right back. Or Umbria? Or the south of France? It's the perfect time of the year for those places.

Dad, it can't be done. Not before the middle of August. Perhaps I could get away for a week then. And please, let's just go to the country and stay there. That will give me a chance to see some people at Yale. I have things I have to do here in June, then I promised Monique and Linda I would take them to the Canadian Rockies, and there are two summer school courses I am supposed to teach.

That was that. The middle of August was less than four months away. With luck, he might still be in working condition.

[III]

SAM WOULD GIVE UP the Rockies at once if he knew his father was dying. The thought that it might be otherwise did not cross Mistler's mind. Then it was his duty to avoid a situation that unjustly put his son in the wrong; he should let Sam know at once. *Quo modo?* Does one say to that thirty-six-year-old son, Look here, correct your seminar papers in the airport lounge and on the plane, or early in the mornings when you are with me and I am still asleep, take that unreformed hippie girlfriend and her gypsy child to Lake Victoria next summer, I am dying, I need the last rites of your physical presence? Could one add — or should one leave unspoken the rest of the message — how deeply it moves the father that this only son's back has begun to stoop, his hairline is in retreat, and his eyes, those eyes, that would throw the father into an abyss of panic and guilt when they filled with tears, look tired behind their glasses? It's only natural, the son spends all day reading. How the father thinks that he — perhaps only he — can still recognize in the son's face the lineaments of the beautiful, fine child? Sam wouldn't let him down. But he might want to kill two birds with one stone. That's it: Monique and Linda have never been back East, let alone to Europe. He would ask his father to include them in the invitation. A brilliant and constructive solution—the family circle-to-be constituted on a moment's notice, and for such a reason too, the future brought into the present, a phoenix rising from the ashes! If Sam made that request, there would be no backing out, on one side or the other, given Sam's determination to make an effort for Monique and Linda. Mistler might as well wait until he was on his deathbed, expecting Sam on the redeye to New York, hoping he wouldn't be late. Wishes are like a pendulum: push the weight in any direction, and it comes back to knock your teeth out. He had to handle this business with Sam right, but it couldn't be done at once. In his misery, Mistler crawled under the hateful brocade, burrowing in the pillows and the splendid, proudly ironed linen sheets. He swallowed one more pill. Like a long shroud, the certainty of sleep stretched before him.

What time was it when he awakened? He had not bothered to unpack the alarm clock; his wristwatch was God knows where, probably in the bathroom, where he had undressed. Seven-thirty! He opened the shutters. Judging by the traffic on the Grand Canal, it was evening—presumably of the day he arrived. He might have slept through the night, but surely not until the evening of the following day. He rummaged in his suitcase, found his bathrobe, and went into the sitting room.

She smiled at him. You've had a good sleep. I am so glad. Do you feel better?

He saw that she had advanced in her book.

What about you? Now you must feel miserable and tired.

No, but I am sad. This book is very sad. It's *Anna Karenina*.

I have done my share of crying over it. When Vronsky breaks Froufrou's back and kicks her. And when Anna can't understand how hard Karenin is trying to patch things up and misses her last chance.

She smiled again and nodded her head.

Would you like a drink? A glass of champagne out of the minibar? I am awfully thirsty, so I will have some water first. Then I'll get ready, and if you haven't any other plans we might go out to dinner.

She also wanted water. They drank their San Pellegrinos in silence.

Now I'll have a real drink, he announced. And you?

No, she was happy as she was. Where had her desire to communicate with him gone?

Then keep on with Tolstoy. I won't be long.

In fact, he took his time, scraping away at his face—he thought it looked no worse than what you'd expect after a tiring flight and a sleep in the afternoon that had been much too long—and then in the bath. His body didn't look bad either. That was all humbug, of course: an old man's face and body are just that, except to the old man himself, when he forgets that he knows better. Enough muscle to attest to his college exertions on the river and a lifelong fondness for tennis and swimming. He wasn't fat. That was all the sweets and butter he hadn't eaten, all the second servings he had refused. Chocolate and *tiramisù*, here I come, he resolved. There wouldn't be enough time for the rubber tire to encircle his middle before he started on the most efficient weight-reduction program known to man. Eat all you want and stay slim—guaranteed success with Dr. Crab's formula or your money back! It would be interesting to see Mr. Julio at work taking in his clothes. Or would the fastidious Mr. Mistler allow himself to look like a long stick draped in floating volumes of cheviot and tweed? A scarecrow—with no patch of corn to guard. Miss Lina might as well taste his ephemeral charms.

All set? he asked. Ready for a trot beyond Campo San Polo, or would you prefer to take the vaporetto? Travel time will be about the same.

There is my suitcase. She giggled. It has these wheels. They're funny on bridges and on cobbles. The boat would be better, though I love to walk. You probably think it's awful to go out to a restaurant with someone pulling a suitcase. But I don't think anybody will take you for a day-tripper.

Mistler considered her. A red cotton cardigan and a lighter red dress that was too long: Why wear such a thing except to hide one's legs? Having seen her in the peignoir he knew she didn't have to. She should be wearing a short skirt; she should be in black. That was something he could fix, if she listened to him.

Ah, your suitcase! I had forgotten about it. That happened to be the truth. Of course, I will be pulling it. And where is your hotel?

I'm not sure you'd call it a hotel. It's more like a room for rent above a pizzeria on the far side of San Giacomo dell'Orio. I think it's clean.

Do you want to stay here? He hesitated, and then added, Until you get used to me, you could sleep on this! He pointed to the fake antique daybed in the living room. Look at all those swell pillows! I wouldn't be surprised if it was comfortable.

She walked over to him, and, with her hands at her side, put her head in the hollow of his shoulder. I'd like you to want me to stay, she said quietly. I don't need any time to get used to you.

Very small ears under that straight brown hair: he turned her face toward him, and found her mouth. It felt immense and tasted sour. Her breath might be worse. She began to moan, and made her mouth even larger. It had an astonishing elasticity, the tongue was also immense—elastic and wide. He began to want, more than anything else she could give, to hold that face between his thighs.

She broke off the kiss.

Please! Let your pants down. You can fuck me later.

His trousers bunched up below his knees, he leaned back in the chair into which she had pushed him. The breasts she exposed were like a little girl's, but flabby, with engorged, spiky nipples. She spread his legs and knelt between them.

Hah! she panted, drive it into my tits. Hard, please God, push harder, real hard, don't be afraid to come. I want you to make me give milk!

This made him more passive. Her face flushed, she grasped herself in one hand and him in the other and ground until a drop of fluid appeared on her nipple.

You see! I can do it. Now, the other one, so it won't be jealous.

More digging. Another drop of murky fluid. She closed her eyes.

One morning, just before Clara stopped nursing Sam, she squeezed milk into his hand and asked him to taste it.

Sweet, isn't it? Would you like it in your tea? she asked.

The taste was sickening, but the feel and look of the milk on his skin aroused him. He took her breast and squeezed it himself.

I'm going to put it in you, he told her. As long as you've got milk, I want you wet with milk when we fuck. Don't you see I want you right now?

. . . .

Memory or instinct? He found the way to the restaurant across bridges and under *sottoporteghi*, following a course that at times seemed to be in circles, although in fact they were advancing, through *rii* that he thought could lead only to the edge of a canal, and, therefore, to a dead end for all but the inhabitants of the one palace that overlooked that canal, but offered instead the possibility of turning left or right into a tiny *campo*, and from there the choice among equally implausible and mysterious *calli* for which the *campo* served as the hub. Except for an occasional figure hurrying toward the railroad station, they were alone. He shifted the arm he had put over her shoulder, unbuttoned the lower part of the back of her dress, slipped his hand between her buttocks, and waited. As he had expected, she thrust her pelvis out to meet him.

You are my guide, she cried hoarsely, always hold me like that. Don't lose me.

She spoke to the owner of the restaurant in an Italian that Mistler found as inelegant as it was rudimentary. When they returned to the hotel, she asked him to take her on the floor. The following day, unprompted, she performed fellatio on him in the green lacquer room of Ca' Rezzonico, which happened to be empty of other tourists. The guard, a girl with thick glasses reading *Oggi*, sat on a folding chair outside the door. Her need to act out sexual fantasies seemed to Mistler insatiable and uncomely, perhaps because they were her fantasies and not his. He oscillated between intense pleasure—he didn't want to, probably wouldn't have been able to, resist this lovemaking that forced every door, and, indeed, he encouraged each new transgression—and an offended detachment from the writhing of their bodies. The questions he put to himself he recognized as stupid. Since by the time of their first copulation he had passed beyond the threshold of curiosity and urgent desire—that happened at the moment of her bizarre attempt at lactation—why was he using, or allowing her to use, his body for these assaults? She made more noise than any woman he had ever known. What did another orgasm, a shriek repeated when he drove harder, add to the sum of pleasure? Why was he willing to pay the price? Her toothbrush, tube of toothpaste, and hairbrush cluttered the edges of both washbasins. When she brushed her teeth, she left globs of toothpaste sometimes enlivened by bits of food adhering to the enamel surfaces. She had hung over the bidet a rubber sack with a tube attached to it that had to be a douche, although he couldn't understand why she needed it; surely she was taking the pill. In the armoires, her clothes were congregating uncontrollably with his. There wasn't a single garment she owned that he liked or that could even evoke in him any sentiment akin to tenderness or pity for a girl whom no one had taught how to dress, and who, in any case, couldn't have afforded the things she might have wanted to have. He suspected that she had no taste at all. He took her to a designer's boutique in the Salizzada San Moisè. Like a homing pigeon, she made for two "outfits" he detested. The saleswoman was an acquaintance of long standing. What did she make of this customer he had brought her?

Why hadn't he asked Clara to come with him to Venice? If he wanted a time of indifference and hazard, why hadn't he dismissed Lina with a pat on that rump he had come to know so well and the promise—so easy to give and fulfill—of assignments from any office of the agency she liked? There wasn't one in Mombasa, but how about Milan or Melbourne? As regular as the tide and just as predictable, Clara met his sexual demands. There wouldn't have been any of the fireworks Lina set off, but the pleasure with Clara when ejaculation approached was fine too, and so was Clara's gratitude when he made love to her, possibly the single benefit of Peter Berry's unforgivable ministrations. No, all things weighed, sex with Lina meant no more to him than sex with Clara, and it brought with it the discomfort of her presence, and the slight sense that he was making a fool of himself. The fact remained that he had not come to Venice without Clara in order to have a sex festival: with Lina or anyone else.

It was also true that, had he brought Clara, he would have had to tell her or endure being nagged. That had become very clear to him. Perhaps not until they had gotten their feet on the ground, for instance on Tuesday over lunch in Torcello, since the place to which they normally went on the Giudecca closed on that day. Afterward, they would have visited Santa Maria Assunta and looked at the *Last Judgment* so that, having made the disclosure, he could contemplate the torments for which his sins qualified him. Telling Clara wasn't going to be easy when he returned to New York either, but there, at least, they would not be in this hermetic intimacy. One bedroom, one sitting room, one bathroom though with the two washbasins; the walk over the Accademia Bridge and across Dorsoduro to the Zattere to catch the vaporetto to the Giudecca; her sense of circumstance, and the show of grief it would dictate; his uncontrollable terror of unpleasantness, her inability to respond to his sadness except by even greater sadness of her own. The devil take it! He had no patience for tragedy. *Evviva* Lina, baseness and farce!

[IV]

It was a perfect day—blue sky and with it cool air of an exhilarating purity. They were getting dressed. Making a moue before the bathroom mirror, Lina had reminded him once again that the reason she had come to Venice remained unchanged. She wanted to photograph him.

Absolutely, he answered, with great pleasure. What would you think of San Michele, after lunch?

Isn't that the cemetery island?

Yes, very quiet during the week. It should be rather beautiful on a day like this.

Because he had gotten into the habit of teasing her, he considered adding, I thought we might do *tableaux mourants* at the graves of Stravinsky and Diaghilev. It's about time someone recognized photography is a society game. I'll help you pose me. Ezra Pound's buried there too: Would you like to present me as Pound? Pound has become respectable. I look more like Pound than Diaghilev or Stravinsky.

He was wearing baggy linen trousers and an open-collared white shirt with broad black stripes under his suede jacket. That costume would do fine, completed by an old-fashioned straw hat from a stall on the Rialto Bridge. The desire to insert his death as a hidden subtext for everything he did or said was becoming irresistible. If she agreed, and the photos had some originality, wackiness—he still didn't know whether she was any good—could they not be published in due course as an elegant, sepia pamphlet: *Death in Venice: A Picture Essay,* with a brief introduction by the late Thomas Hooker Mistler III? Provided, of course, whoever owned the Thomas Mann copyright didn't object. Close-ups of his face, shots that showed him cavorting among the graves, et cetera, would alternate with material on how, all the while, his liver was going down the drain. The medical illustrations could be supplied by Katz Imaging Associates of East Seventy-second Street, with the permission of the estate of the aforesaid Mr. Mistler. That was easy; he would require his executors to grant it, in a codicil to his last will. What with the modest celebrity he had attained in his lifetime, the public's interest in the most murderous forms of cancer, and, above all, the nastiness of the concept, which "the age demanded," the pamphlet might be a runaway success. An exhibition at the MoMA, or in the worst case at the Whitney, would not be out of the question. He should reveal to Lina the potential scope of the project. Anyway, why bother with keeping up the pretense? She would be sorry the moment he told her, and perhaps for an hour or two afterward, but hardly grief stricken. That was the basic advantage of her presence over Clara's. Men's coarse humor, self-abasement, humiliation—her acquaintance with all of these seemed extensive. Assuming that the way he treated her left a trace in her memory, it was bound to be banal and transient; he was willing to bet that very quickly she would confuse it with the outrageous behavior of another man, perhaps Gansevoort. The real danger was that knowing his situation might make her want—feel obliged?—to fuck even harder. The paradox was amusing: that he, who had so little time, should have less and less inclination to seize the day. Had anyone put the question to him in the time of his innocence, for instance on some occasion when he was seated under the honeysuckle bower at Crow Hill, hot from a set of tennis, enjoying his draft of gin, he would have surely given the exactly wrong answer. He would have said something about wanting, before he took his final bow, to try every kind of sexual experience—weird, round-the-clock copulation, like those festivals of horror movies one used to see advertised on marquees of theaters near Times Square. It turned out instead that sex before death excited him about as much as going to a business lunch. He would rather eat a tuna-salad sandwich at his desk in the office.

Running a very large business had taught Mistler that decisions on most matters can and should be postponed. Thus, the Sun King had made a habit of countering petitions with *Nous verrons*. An explanation to Lina could be postponed, certainly until they were comfortably settled on the restaurant terrace and had ordered drinks and lunch. It was already half past one, and they had to get themselves over to the Giudecca.

If we are to believe that the need for such a talk arose out of the plans to prepare a pamphlet on Mr. Mistler as one of the walking dead, it disappeared while they waited for the vaporetto to take them across the canal from the Zattere. It turned out that there would be no *tableaux vivants* or *mourants*, because the modest church on San Michele, tombs of illustrious artists, and high-growing weeds—Lina had been to the island and remembered it accurately, although she didn't mention among its characteristics the ambient smell of something like dog shit that Mistler recollected so clearly from his most recent visit—were the opposite of what she wanted. She had thought of a setting that was aquatic and, therefore, Venetian, but with the water invisible. Venice was to be inferred: therefore, no ogives or bridges, and no gargoyles peeking from a capital.

Light like this—but indirect—and nothing to distract one from your face, she said. I love your face. You have the most beautiful, wise face in the world.

Will a background of lines with wash hanging from them be satisfactory? And walls that seem endless and blind? Then we should go to Fondamente Nuove.

Beautiful. There will be shade?

He had come to realize that Lina's understanding of how Venice fitted on the compass was limited. Yes, he told her, and at the same time you can count on steady, strong light, because it will reflect off the lagoon.

For the second day in a row, he allowed himself a sherbet. He had drunk most of the carafe of Prosecco. Obviously, there were some experiences he did not mind repeating and accumulating. It was a pity that his unseemly craving for sweets was so much greater than his appetite for Lina's body! Four Italian men in business suits had shifted their chairs and were staring at her without attempting to conceal their interest by any of the maneuvers to which he might have resorted when so engaged. Two of them had unbuttoned their shirts. One wore a gold chain. It was possible that a religious medal, presumably the Virgin, suspended from it was nestling against more hair farther down, in the vicinity of the navel. Could his own lack of enthusiasm about Lina and the prospect of her ministrations be ascribed to an abrupt and general decline of his libido? If so, it was an unexpected symptom. He felt tired, and stiff in the joints, even though he had been getting plenty of sleep. Wasn't that quite enough to drive the point home to him?

She was wearing her photographer-on-assignment clothes: black jeans, a shirt and a sweater she had borrowed from him, beige socks, and the highly polished brown shoes that laced like a man's he had talked her into buying. Dressed like this, she looked all right; the trick was to keep her from getting fancy. She had caught on that it wasn't necessary to talk at him all the time. Had she not been there, he would have had his lunch alone, reading the *Herald Tribune* between courses. In that respect, the presence at his table of this young woman was an improvement. Since their first session, she had asked for nothing in their lovemaking that he found repulsive. When they returned to the hotel, it would be time for a late siesta. Then too he might be glad to have her around.

We've stumbled into being good companions, he told her.

In fact, he was more than ever convinced that she had carefully planned the invasion.

Is this a good way to spend a week? he continued. I mean, will it be when you look back on it? And what happens when I go back to New York? Is your job in Paris still on?

She had been asking with increasing frequency whether she could do her telephoning from the bedroom without interfering with calls he was expecting or wanted to make. In the freelance business, having to make lots of calls is usually a bad sign. He had begun to fear that her next assignment had fallen through or was in peril.

The Brazilian couple wants me to start a few days later, because the contractor is late finishing the apartment, but that's all right. *Vogue* has something I can do while I wait. So I won't be just hanging out. Oh, Thomas, I wanted to be with you. I wanted it as soon as I saw you at the party. But I'm not sure that you are pleased with me. You seem so sad, almost distant.

I'm sorry. That's the impression I usually give except when I'm hard at work. Then I forget how everything I have done is subject to question, could have been done some other way, and on and on. You shouldn't take it personally. I'm not depressed or even unhappy. In fact, I used to consider myself a rather happy man. Or maybe I should say lucky. The trouble is that even special moments—in recent years they mostly have had to do with my son, Sam—don't make me cheerful. They just sit there—at a distance.

That's awful!

It could be a lot worse! My father suffered from depressions. Right after the war, when he came back from Europe, and toward the end of his life. That last bout was connected to some grotesque events in his business. I know how depression can make one suffer, and I haven't experienced anything like it—ever. Let's head for the Fondamente. And apropos of nothing, if you need an assignment after Paris, or sometime later, give my partner Jack Newcomb a call. He is at the New York office. It's better than going through me. I'll tell Jack to give you every chance.

They took the number 5 line, making an enormous loop. Prosecco and red made a nice combination. Perhaps during the rest of the stay he should walk less, use water transportation more, not just to cross the Grand Canal or go from the Zattere over to the Giudecca, and step up the consumption of great wines. There were so many reds he had never drunk. It wasn't as though he ran any risk of cirrhosis. How pleasantly easy it was to make Lina grateful. Which had meant more to her: the promise of employment or that he had taken her into his confidence? It had to be the former. She was a poor kid from somewhere in Brooklyn or Queens—that was his guess, she had told him nothing about her childhood—and probably had less than five thousand dollars in her savings account, and payments due on her credit card.

They were on the sunny side of the deck, in the space between the passenger cabin and the bridge. She stood behind him and held him in such a tight embrace that he felt her nipples and mons through their clothes. Familiar palaces came into view and slowly disappeared. Everything was very predictable. The vaporetto kept to the printed schedule, docking and casting off. Smooth, well-practiced maneuvers: the engine thrown into reverse churning the water, the bump when the ship lurched against the platform; the *marinaio*, who was also the ticket collector, having stored his over-the-shoulder black leather bag with tickets and cash in the bridge cabin and pulled on his work gloves, looped the frayed hemp line over a cleat the size of a small anvil, tied a perfect figure-eight knot and then untied it, fiddled with the sliding barrier. His fine voice called out the name of the stop, and then *Permesso, permesso!* as passengers poured out and others embarked. Venetians of all categories: thin-lipped ladies in gray or black, artisans carrying clunky tools of their trade or fixtures they were going to install somewhere or other, an occasional musician with an instrument, schoolchildren. Foreign students in sandals, hiking boots, or complicated dirty running shoes, smelling of stale food and staggering under rucksacks. Retirees with their money and documents in belts like marsupia. The occasional elegant couple, of undefinable age, distinguished, dressed in silk, khaki, cashmere, and suede—one such couple was examining Mistler and Lina with evident amusement. He was sure they were French, of the right sort. Lina had remained glued to him. Her hand was under his shirt. The distinguished-looking lady whispered something into her companion's ear. It was probably the equivalent of—Look at that old satyr. Clara might have said the same, and he would have nodded agreement. A *fou rire* overcame him. He took hold of Lina's wrist and got her to tease his nipples. Let the nice couple have a good look. He had just remembered that, in the Mistler family, he did not have a monopoly on indiscretions.

[V]

SHORTLY AFTER it became clear that Mistler, Berry & Lovett had not only gotten off the ground but was well on its way to becoming "hot," Mistler's uncle Samuel Abthorp invited him to lunch at the grandest of his uptown clubs, for membership in which he had coincidentally arranged to have Mistler proposed and irresistibly supported. It was understood that he was, and had always been, Mr. Abthorp's favorite nephew. They finished their turkey hash. Sometime during the pause that preceded the serving of the muskmelon, his uncle said he wished to state a point of view about Mistler, Berry, one he suggested that Mistler might do worse than keep in mind. This tiny bit of emphasis was unnecessary. The nephew knew that the uncle's advice on anything concerning business was a commodity both delicate and precious, normally offered only to certain titans of industry who understood that the great man's observations—for instance about the way the market was acting up, the activities of a cash-rich and secretive company mining diamonds in South Africa—which he might put forward in his offhand, almost indifferent manner, deserved to be taken as revealed truth, and to be rewarded, without prompting, for Mr. Abthorp would not think of asking for any compensation, by some elegant sign of respect and friendship. One might, for instance, offer the lead underwriter's slot to Mr. Abthorp's investment bank in a large issue of securities, or request that he personally devise and carry out the scheme involving the South African mining giant.

Money is being made constantly in this country, everywhere and by all sorts of people, said the uncle. People that you, or your poor father, or I had never heard of when they started out, and might not have particularly liked at the time. A great deal of money. That's why American business will continue to be strong. But most of the money ends up being controlled in New York, by a very small group of men. Some bankers, of course. Men who sit on investment committees. Eventually, when the new people really have a lot of money, they too want to be inside the circle of control, out of pride and to be safe. They look for an opening, but the positions where power is exercised are filled. Pretty much permanently. By people like you and me, and people we have always known. Then the new men figure out that the next best thing is to get close to the men who are inside, and they try to make themselves useful in some activity. The more useful the better. They understand that men who run important institutions will think twice before they kick a big donor in the teeth. These new men look around, read annual reports, see who is where. There are consultants for this sort of thing. Pretty soon, they see that it all comes down to two museums, the opera, a couple of hospitals, the botanical garden, and the zoo. Perhaps the library. Oh, there is fund-raising for the universities, but few of those new people have been to Harvard or Yale, so that's a road seldom taken. The boards of the other institutions are like waiting clubs; you don't join them if you can help it. The new men go on giving money, and then more money, and if they are presentable, you know, able to fit in, and if they stay rich, they may get on one of the right boards—or at least some sort of advisory council to study baboons or Turkish toilets. I want to see you on the boards that count. You will need to work hard as a new member, and the agency will have to give some money. It's more efficient than dipping into your own pocket. But not very much money, because you are who you are. There's no quota against you. You understand I'm not suggesting that you need the prestige, like the other fellows. No one is going to cut your loan lines. But you should be in places where you will become known to the new men with big new money. They'll probably come to think you're pretty bright. And they will tend to believe they need you, because they'll see you as one of the keepers of the gates they want to crash. Their companies don't have established relationships with the older advertising agencies, and can hire you for major campaigns. If you agree, I'll mention here and there that you are interested in doing something for the community and are available. In fact, I have already spoken to Newt Richardson about you. He expects you to call.

The nephew grasped the wisdom of the uncle's words and the likelihood that the subject would never be raised again so directly.

Uncle Samuel, he said, I have a partner, Peter Berry. He's a sort of cousin. You know him, I'm quite sure. Peter is more gregarious than I. Could you put in a word for him as well? We do everything that concerns the agency together.

That's the fellow you roomed with at college. I remember him. Can't say I like his father. He hangs around the bar at the club a bit too much. Never amounted to anything. You have put that young fellow's name on the agency's door, but when people talk about your shop they talk about Mistler. Not about Berry.

He's been a good friend, Uncle. I wouldn't have started out without him.

That's your business then. Make him your own project.

So be it. Mistler followed Uncle Abthorp's advice, but soon the restive nephew began to chafe and yawn. If a decision was to be made, he wanted it made swiftly—by himself. The board meetings of cultural institutions were a tribulation that ate up time he would have sooner spent at the agency—or, in fact, anywhere else. It turned out, though, that the project of inserting his partner into these august bodies did not require an immense effort. Mistler was discovering the extent of his own prestige. It was also true that men not so discriminating as Mr. Abthorp—or perhaps simply less stuffy—did not nec-essarily look down their noses at Peter or his hapless parent. According to the established order of things, he fit in. Besides, Peter swam in not-for-profit waters like a catfish in a warm, murky pond. To avoid offending his uncle, Mistler dutifully stuck to the boards of the opera and of the hospital where he was born and, as it now seemed certain, would soon utter his last cry of pain—unless he outsmarted Dr. Hurley and man-aged to die at home.

The rest of the New York do-gooders—and real estate developers and cleaned-up Texans—they're all yours, he told Peter. Have fun!

Some trading of the properties on their Monopoly board was required when Mistler married Clara. He wanted her position in New York to be brilliant. Husband and wife are one; in Mistler's opinion, she should have her pick of the prebends within the agency's gift. Therefore, with some effort—she was so young and inexperienced in the ways of charity—Mistler arranged for Clara to replace him at the hospital. This he considered a favor from her to him: he had none of the Mistler family enthusiasm for doctors or their patients. Clara didn't object to the hospital, but principally she liked animals—even more than carnivorous plants. That settled the issue. Peter had to step aside for Clara, although he too was fond of the zoo. The transfer was made without a stumble, since Peter was finding it increasingly difficult to oppose Mistler on any issue. Mistler meanwhile had learned that announcing to Peter what he wanted done was more efficient than the two-hour lunches at which they had previously thrashed out problems. The result, in the end, was the same.

As the early years of Mistler's marriage to Clara went by, he was pleased to conclude that he had, in general, done well by her. She had the baronial duplex she wanted, a growing collection of first-rate Philadelphia furniture and silver, and a garden at Crow Hill that had been redesigned by an Englishman at a cost that would have made even her late mother-in-law blanch. All these good things had been deserved. She made no trouble. She was the mother of Sam. Her beauty continued to be the best in its genre. Under Mistler's relentless tutelage, she had learned to dress. Photographs of her appeared in *Vogue* and *Town and Country,* and in Mistler, Berry ads for the British Tourist Board, Swiss chocolate, and the most dignified of credit cards. Within the bounds of notions about making love she had acquired at Smith, she was available when he needed her. Mistler didn't wish her to experiment. The other sort of thing was exciting, sometimes he couldn't resist it, but, in his opinion, not appropriate in a marriage, not for the long haul. One shouldn't get used to eating very spicy food at every meal.

Peter and Jill Berry divorced. It was Jill's idea; she left with a man who had been the golf pro at their country club in Locust Valley. According to Peter, the man must have been stuffing her in the storage room over the pro shop for some time, long enough for her to be quite sure she liked it. Out of the blue, he was offered a better-paying job by a resort in Hawaii. He wasn't about to say no to the salary or the climate, and she didn't want to give up the sex. The alimony and child support she asked of Peter were ample but not excessive; considering the size of her own fortune, she didn't need them, and living with a golf pro or even marrying him wouldn't put a dent in her social standing. The arrangements were concluded without fuss and in record time, and they included Jill's having custody of the twin girls who were at Chapin. Mistler was surprised that Peter hadn't made an effort to keep them in New York. There should have been some chance of it in this amiable business transaction.

I travel too much. You keep opening all these new offices, said Peter, and when I'm in the city the hours at work are too long and getting worse. Why should I try to take them from Jill? So they can be brought up by a governess?

There was a small grain of good sense in this, but it didn't alter Mistler's conviction that Peter spent more time on cultural trips for museum trustees than on a vice-chairman's normal responsibility of visiting foreign offices, and that his business hours seldom extended beyond six o'clock. Peter's diminishing interest in work, however, was a problem Mistler preferred not to think about, and the sacrifices Peter should be willing to make to have those girls with him were definitely not Mistler's affair. Perhaps, in his gypsy way, Peter was right. The beach in Hawaii could be a nice place for little ten-year-olds. According to agency gossip, the golf pro was a decent fellow. In addition to being blessed with superior pectorals and a bulging crotch, he could occasionally slog his way through a reading project, the text being most often *Popular Mechanics*. In the end, none of this really mattered. Peter had been Mistler's college roommate and the best man in his wedding: there would always be a place set for him at the Mistlers' for dinner in town, and a bedroom at his disposal in the country. It helped that Clara hadn't cared for Jill's Oyster Bay airs, and, instead, had always had a soft spot in her heart for Peter.

One benefit of the debacle—Peter had responded with indifference to an attempt to pair him off with Mistler's attractive and rich first cousin on his father's side and, for all Mistler knew, to the onslaught of various members of the agency's female personnel—was Peter's availability to escort Clara about town when Mistler was away, which happened at least every other week, and when he refused to attend certain functions. These included most cocktail parties, because they started too early, just as he was hitting his stride at the office, liberated from the telephone and visitors, and all dinners to benefit good causes, because they also started early and he had to struggle, sometimes unsuccessfully, not to fall asleep during the speeches. It was nice that Clara need not rely exclusively on the agency's two best-looking fairy copywriters to be her escorts, although they had the advantage of being always free and, in addition, excellent company. Particularly at benefits, Peter Berry was more useful. He knew everybody.

In the spring of the year after Peter's divorce, the zoo organized a trip to Borneo for members of its board, spouses, and a handful of the largest donors. Like most such trips, it was to start officially in London. After twelve days on the island looking at wildlife and authentic primitive villages, there would be a stop in Singapore and return via Paris. Clara had always been mad about orangutans.

We're going, she announced at dinner as soon as the dates had been fixed. And then I want to spend a few days in Paris and have a dreamy time eating white asparagus and foie gras.

He had rather expected this.

Sweetie, you're going, and you'll bring back lots of photos and try to make sure the foie gras doesn't stick to your ribs. You know I can't possibly get away. We'll be smack in the middle of the presentation to Nabisco—we badly need to get the rest of their business—and I expect to be negotiating the purchase of Durant's Montreal office. Just think of it! If we're successful, we'll cover all of Canada. Besides, if I went with you, we would both be away for more than three weeks in a row. I know Melinda is an angel, but wouldn't it be less dreary for Sam if I was here?

You're never here even when you are here.

That's because I have you, and I don't need to worry about the kid. You'll see. I'll make a special, supreme effort.

What you mean is that you think I shouldn't go.

No, that's not it at all. In fact, as your sponsor and Rasputin at the zoo, I order you to go and to have a first-rate time!

Well, I can't. I've checked. There isn't one woman going alone. Even Emmy de Groot—that was the honorary chairwoman of the board whose husband had recently died—is bringing her cousin, Woolly Hitchcock. Jane Cruikshank isn't coming. She hasn't been well. So that's that. No Borneo and no orangutans, all for the greater glory of Mistler, Berry &

Lovett! You know, by the way, if you are worried about Sam, we could make the trip shorter. By skipping Paris and maybe even Singapore.

I am heartbroken about this, but really I can't. You have given me a brilliant idea, though, with old Woolly Hitchcock. You know that he was a friend of Father's. Why not invite Peter? It is only fair. He has never stopped regretting that he had to get off that board. He'll go with you like a shot.

Why doesn't he have to work?

I do it for him.

Oh well.

Of course Clara came around and Peter agreed. Before they left, Peter presented Mistler with an old and ingenious wood netsuke of three monkeys.

Here, he said, probably these are more pleasant at close quarters than the live ones. See no evil, hear no evil, speak no evil! I really appreciate this.

Clara returned from the trip radiant and tender. He noticed it when she was with Sam, in the attention she paid to the flowers in the house, and also in bed, although she was often too sleepy and whispered how they should make a date for the weekend. Momentarily, he worried that she had caught one of those exotic amoebae that linger in the system and wear you out, but there was no fever and no other symptoms.

In the middle of the summer, when Clara and Sam had moved to Crow Hill, Mistler went to Paris on a Monday, giving himself enough time to get through a series of meetings and still return for the weekend. On his first free evening, he dined with Madame Portes. She was in town, between the festivals in Aix-en-Provence and Salzburg. They sat under the linden tree in her garden, the existence of which one would not guess passing before the severe beige building in the rue de Lille on the ground floor of which was her apartment. She had hardly changed; he wondered whether she ever would. The maze of hair in which the senior Mr. Mistler had lost his heart was untouched by gray, her posture was straight and majestic, her skin without blemish except on those large, strong hands that no longer had the aspect of a young girl's. She spoke to him about the staging of the *Così Fan Tutte* she had just seen, and also the quality of the voices, which had not completely satisfied her.

It is a diabolical opera, Thomas, she concluded, and it is all so much like life. One is always betrayed, especially when there is only reason to be trusting. Mozart was younger than you when he died, but he knew these dreadful truths so well. I wonder whether you do.

He adored her voice, her speech formed by the most careful of English nannies and long acquaintance with well-bred Americans, and the way her laughing eyes fixed one when she spoke.

He was a genius!

True. But he had also paid particularly close attention to women. Before his legs could touch the floor when he sat at table. I don't think you have been as attentive.

He hadn't gone to boarding school. Remember how you thought it was dreadful? I didn't know any women.

Of course. What a silly way to educate boys. Thomas, I saw your wife in Paris in May.

Really! Clara never told me. How odd.

I mean quite literally that I saw her. She didn't see me. It was at the Pré Catalan, in the dusk. She was with Peter Berry.

Of course. They were in Paris together, after the zoo's trip to Borneo. You should have sent over a message. Clara would have been so pleased.

Thomas, *ils se tenaient très mal.* Forgive me. I don't wish to meddle. An adventure or two won't hurt a good marriage. One should be willing to close one's eyes, if necessary. But this man isn't just your friend. He is your partner.

The butler served orangeade. It was time to go. Tante Elisabeth, he asked, why did you love Dad so much?

Because he was like you, Thomas.

And afterward?

Ah, *e poi, e poi.* . . . Come back to see me soon.

Mistler returned to New York on Friday in midafternoon as scheduled and asked to be driven directly to the country. On the way, with almost total concentration, he read the office mail his secretary had given to the driver. Clara and Sam waited for him on the front lawn. At day camp, Sam had learned to throw a baseball. It had been a fine summer. Except for the ridge of Sam's nose, which was peeling, his tan and Clara's were perfect. Mistler told the driver to take the bags to the bedroom, and he and Sam played catch until the first mosquitoes. Clara watched them. They had planned to celebrate his return by having dinner early, with Sam, and there was just enough time for Mistler to take a bath and change. When Clara had sent Sam to bed, Mistler asked her to sit with him on the back porch. They drank brandy. It was still light enough to see the white hydrangeas, which were in full bloom. The lawn smelled of fresh mowing. Out at its edge, very young rabbits were nibbling on something or other as though they had never heard of Farmer Brown. The idea that he might permit Peter Berry to spoil the order of his life was preposterous.

Clara, he said, I understand you are sleeping with Peter. Does that mean that you intend to leave with him, like Jill?

She didn't answer, but it seemed to him that her chin was trembling.

That was a cheap crack.

He nodded his head.

Who told you about it?

It doesn't matter. The answer to my question is important. I will take back the crack about Jill, but I'd like to have an answer now, if possible.

Well, no. We haven't really talked about it. Thomas, I was having a sweet, careless time, you never pay attention, I didn't think you'd find out. I am so sorry, Thomas. I don't want to leave.

And I don't want you to go. The business between you and Peter is over from this very minute. The business between you and me will take more time. I will deal with Peter on Monday. I warn you. You are not to speak to him at all until he and I have talked.

What will you do to him?

Nothing violent, I assure you. Now go to bed please.

He slept that night in a guest room, but the next night he slept with her, paying great attention, intent on discovering what she might have learned from Peter or invented to make Peter happy. It was possible that her caresses had grown slower and more intelligent. The improvement, even if it was due to Peter, was welcome. However, it was also possible that she was making a special effort, in order to be forgiven.

The prospect of throwing Peter out of the firm was wonderfully tempting. Nothing in their agreements gave him the right to do that, and yet he supposed that Peter would obey, if ordered to leave. But his shares in the agency would have to be bought. If the agency came up with the cash, there were projects that would have to be abandoned or postponed, perhaps for a long time. Of course, he could buy Peter out himself. The trouble was that the agency had become too valuable. He would have to liquidate most of his other investments, and perhaps borrow as well. In addition, with the purchase of the Canadian agency negotiated but not yet signed, and some other transactions that were less advanced, he didn't like the idea of a cantankerous separation. It wouldn't matter so far as the agency's work or existing client relations were concerned, since Peter had no important following, but outsiders, prospective clients, might not understand the event's true lack of importance. No, it wasn't a good time for the beheading of Peter. It was also possible that being bought out at a negotiated price was a solution Peter might quite like, once he was told that Mistler knew about him and Clara and realized that life at Mistler's side would be more unpleasant than in the past. The spigot of cultural tourism turned off, courtesy of Mistler, closer supervision of his expense account, especially of large sums spent at uptown hotels in New York. Mistler would fix Peter's wagon, but somewhat differently. He would make him leave in due course, but it would be at a time of Mistler's choosing, and arranged so that the agency bought his shares at book value, not for what they were really worth.

On Monday morning, he arrived at the agency before eight, asked to be called as soon as Mr. Berry came in, and read through the papers Miss Tuck had not considered important enough to send to him with his driver. By nine o'clock, he was attending to current business. At ten, Miss Tuck told him Mr.

Berry had telephoned to say he would be late, because he was stuck in traffic.

All right, he answered, please ask him to come in as soon as he does arrive.

It was quarter of eleven when Berry, long and slim, coffee mug in hand, decked out in seersucker trousers and embroidered suspenders, white button-down shirt, and a club bow tie, appeared in his office. He rested his right buttock on the corner of Mistler's desk.

Good time in Paris? How would you like some real coffee? I'll get my secretary to bring you a mug.

Thanks, no coffee. I had the meetings with Publicis and later Havas, and we are all right on both fronts. Then, quite unexpectedly, I found out about you and Clara. That's a betrayal, Peter. It had never occurred to me that I couldn't trust you.

Berry got off Mistler's desk and stood up with his hands on the back of a chair.

That's right. It just happened. She is very beautiful. You are so used to her, you probably don't realize how beautiful and attractive. I am sorry. What else can I say except that, of course, I will offer to marry her if that's what you wish.

You will not offer Clara anything, you and she are through. I require you to have no contact with her at all, except in public, with other people present. The more interesting issue is your future at this firm. The way you are working less and less, your future seems uncertain. So far as dealings between you and me go, inside the agency I plan to treat you as I always have, but I don't want to see you anywhere else if it can be avoided. For instance, I want you to resign from the Arcadia—

when I walk into the club, I don't want to have to ask myself whether you are at the members' table. And watch your step here. I'll be watching too.

Peter had turned very red. Just as Mistler was asking himself whether a stroke was in the making, or whether that extraordinary color was only the combined effect on very fair skin of anger and too much time in the sun, Peter spoke: Have it your way, Thomas, with Clara and in all your other little projects.

He paused at the door, and turning back toward Mistler added, You do know that you've always been a prick. That's why I don't feel the least bit of guilt toward you.

Hah! As an example of how one recollection can lead to another, this wasn't bad. Here he was, seated on a chair borrowed from the minuscule shop that wasn't quite a bar, looking over the water into the distance—at San Michele, to be precise—with the shade on the Fondamente Nuove growing dense while Lina alternated between arranging his pose and shooting, and suddenly he remembered.

I've got it, he told her. I was sure I would. I know where I met that Frenchman who was looking at us down his nose.

What do you mean?

Oh, on the vaporetto. The elegant couple who got on at San Alvise. Didn't you notice how they disapproved of an old man like me being hugged and tickled under his shirt by a beautiful young girl?

I wasn't tickling you. You were guiding my hand and I was doing something a whole lot nicer. Stop talking now, and try, just try, a small smile.

Click, click, click. Pursuit of the perfect shot, obtained by chance.

That's what the Frenchman thought too. But he didn't think I deserved it. The man's name is Simonnet. Arnaud Simonnet. He's the president of the French investment bank that arranged the purchase of our French agency. The woman is his wife. I've had dinner at their home. How funny that I didn't recognize them right away.

Are you worried that they will talk?

Not especially. They live in Paris, they don't see the same people as Clara and I, they won't have a chance to tell the story to anyone who would be interested. Though once I found out something that was both interesting and important to me through just that sort of coincidence.

You mean gossip!

No, in that case the person who told me really cared, I mean wanted to help.

Who was it?

The most wonderful woman in the world. She met my father in France before Paris was liberated, and never stopped loving him. Now she's dead too. Otherwise she would be in love even today. Have you almost finished?

I haven't, but there isn't enough light.

Good! Let's go to the Gesuiti. Do you know it? No? It's an amazing late-baroque church that's never open when you expect it to be, but this could be the right hour to get in. We'll take a route that is illogical, and not the shortest, but pretty. I just hope they aren't in the middle of a service.

Aren't you going to tell me what this woman said to you?

Certainly not. That would be a double indiscretion.

He slung one of her camera bags over his shoulder and guided her along the Fondamente in the direction of the Sacca della Misericordia. Then they turned away from the lagoon, zigzagged through working-class streets, crossed first one canal and then another, each time coming face-to-face with a huge palace, and absurdly turned back toward the lagoon. All at once, on the right, the church was before them, austere and unwelcoming.

We're all right, he said to Lina. Look, the door within the door. It's open. Call it today's miracle.

A guardian was surely sleeping in the sacristy. Otherwise, they were alone. Lina genuflected and crossed herself. Jeez, she whispered. What is this gray-and-white stuff? Is it silk?

Touch it, it's marble. Wonderfully inlaid and worked and smoothed to look like silk. Or wallpaper. It's like nothing I have seen anywhere else.

I want to walk around.

Do. You can leave your bag. I'll wait for you here.

He sat down before the first side altar on the left. An adept of ultra-rapid visits, she returned in no time at all. Mistler put a five-hundred-lira piece into the box that turned on the light projectors, thinking they might rivet her attention, although, in reality, the projectors were so badly placed that on such a clear afternoon they only made the light less pleasant. After a moment he asked, What do you think?

It's really something. Hey, I want to shoot it.

I think that's forbidden. But you could look at the painting through your zoom lens. It's more powerful than my binoculars.

She screwed an enormous tube onto her Nikon, peered through it, and said, I wish there were more color, or light. It's hard to read. What are they doing to that man down on the left?

Roasting him and making sure the liver is well done.

Come on, Thomas!

I mean it. It's Saint Lawrence on the grill, the patron of cooks. The painting had to be dark, that's Titian's fidelity to the legend, but I suppose Titian would have wanted to have it dark anyway. He was a relatively young man when he began it—no older than Gansevoort or I! It took about ten years to complete. By then, he wasn't looking at the world through rose-colored glasses. Remember the *Pietà*, the very dark Titian you liked in the Accademia? We saw it yesterday. Those two paintings are quite alike—one and the same cry of despair.

What happened to Saint Lawrence? I mean the legend?

He was a fervent Christian, who had the bad luck to live during the reign of Emperor Decius, a rough type mostly known for trying to turn the clock back. A pagan fundamentalist. There were more and more Christians in the Roman Empire. To all those he could lay his hands on, he gave the choice between abjuring Christianity and martyrdom. Lawrence was brought to Decius at night, and Decius said, Sacrifice to the gods, or the night will end for you in pain. Lawrence gave an answer that was something like: My night is not made of darkness. It's bathed in eternal light. That didn't amuse Decius, and he called for the grill. See? The contraption that looks like a camp bed without a mattress. The man lying on it and looking wretched is the saint, and the man who seems to be holding him up by the shoulders, and really looks just as uncomfortable as Lawrence—probably because of the heat—he must be one of the torturers. Then you have the helpful fellow crouching on the ground, blowing on the coals to make sure they stay hot, and, on the other side, the burly type with the huge cooking fork is poking at Lawrence's liver.

Jeez!

You put it so well. They're doing the Lord's work. Totally absorbed in it, the torturers and the saint. Look, the contrast with the other figures is striking. For instance, the two intellectuals, above to the right. Very distant. They might be discussing poetry. I am fascinated by the intense light at the very top of the painting: Is it a painterly effect, an electric storm, or the Holy Ghost peeking through the clouds, making sure the Lord's work is being done correctly? Take a good look! I'll put in another coin.

She stared at him rather queerly, but he did not intend to be interrupted. The light clicked back on.

It could be the Holy Ghost, because of the intensity of the light, Mistler continued, but I have my doubts. I haven't noticed that it's a part of religious iconography to have the Father or the Son attend torture sessions of the martyrs. In fact, right now I can't think of any painting of the crucifixion or the deposition where the Father or the Holy Ghost looks on. And they're not in on any of the preliminaries either—the Son being whipped or crowned with thorns, or lugging the cross up the Via Dolorosa. They are absent. One wonders why. Celestial squeamishness? Or is it respect for the logic of the faithful? Fear that belief might be strained beyond the breaking point if the Father actually observed such things being done to the Son and did nothing to stop them? Even with the Son's tortured body right before him? Of course, at the Last Judgment, the Son is always there, enthroned, dispensing justice, which means torture for most people, and the Father usually looks on. Why does the Father look on then? To make sure the Son doesn't begin to feel pity, when he remembers what the Father had arranged to have done to him? To put his stamp of approval on the Son's justice and its consequences?

Thomas, stop! How can you say these men are doing the Lord's work? That's disgusting.

Which? My saying that it's the Lord's work or what these people are doing?

Both. According to the story you just told me, it was the emperor who ordered the torture.

She wiped a tear from her eye.

Well, we obviously agree that it's bad to roast people on a grill. But why isn't it the Lord's work? Who organized it, who programmed Decius, if not the Lord? Doesn't everything happen according to his design?

People do bad things. They do them against God's wishes.

I know that explanation, but I can't get away from the thought that if an omnipotent God exists, it is his will being done. Take a man with a liver cancer. Isn't it God's will that he should have it? Of course, you might say that it's advance payment for his sins. Or for Adam's sin — and let's not forget Eve. Certainly you don't dispute that he must at least allow these things to be done. What's the difference between willing evil and allowing it to go on, if you have the power to stop it?

There is free will. Human beings have free will.

That's the right answer, according to the church, but I have never been able to accept it. Anyway, it doesn't apply to the poor fellow with a cancer on his liver. Why is he being punished before he was judged? He is still alive, he might repent. Hah! You must know the proper procedures for repentance and forgiveness better than I. So why not wait at least until the guy has been judged before sticking the crab into his body? Or why roast this saint who wasn't a bad man? I know the standard answer: He is being roasted for the greater glory of God. Balls! There is a beautifully comic side to the free-will theory, you know. It's like saying that characters in a play have free will. The actors try to trick you into thinking that, but every word they speak, every action—everything that happens in the play—was in fact ordered by the playwright. For instance, in *King Lear:* Cornwall doesn't decide to pluck Gloucester's eyes out. Shakespeare decided it, based on histories he read and his own observation of how things are done in this world. That's how it is with God and free will. Ha! Ha!

She hissed at him. I don't think it's right to talk like that in a church. Let's get out of here. Besides, you are really morbid. Why do you say it's the saint's liver that man is poking? That's disgusting. I think it's his buttocks or his side.

You may have a point there. Come to think of it, isn't one's liver on the right side, the side away from the fork? Never mind. I seem to have liver on my brain.

He was tempted to say, You see, I have a right to be morbid and unreasonable and blasphemous. The fellow with the cancer, that's me. I found out about it, that I will die quite soon, late in the afternoon before Anna Williams's party, just before you and I met. Shush! It's a big secret. Only my doctors and my lawyer know about it. But he couldn't bring himself to speak about it. Not yet.

[VI]

I'D LIKE SOMETHING SWEET, an ice cream.

Her voice was surly. To his own surprise, instead of irritation he felt a vague need to make amends, almost to propitiate.

There isn't any place right here. Are you willing to undertake a ten-minute walk?

Yes, if you carry both camera bags.

He thought that once again he had chosen an absurd itinerary, an absurd destination. He would treat her to gelati in a café looking on the equestrian statue of Colleoni, the huge brick pile of Santi Giovanni e Paolo, and, beyond the church, the trompe l'oeil facade of the *scuola* that had become the municipal hospital and housed a collection of antique surgical instruments. How did those differ from instruments of torture? In the purpose for which they were intended. Were the ones now in use in the operating rooms of the hospital where Hurley & Co. wanted him to become a lodger less terrifying? No, but anesthesia had been perfected. While "the wounded surgeon plies the steel that questions the distempered part," the patient floats in a sea of nightmares. Although there were surely countless others of the same sort nearer the Gesuiti and more generally on the way to the hotel, he was leading Lina to this particular café, the name of which he did not know or had forgotten, but whose location he knew exactly by reason of his regular visits to the Bellinis and the Veroneses in the church. He was hoping that when they finally reached it, the establishment would have a familiar and comfortable feeling. It didn't. They sat down at a table in the *campo*. A waiter sauntered over, summoned by vigorous gestures, and Mistler ordered a vanilla ice cream for Lina and a coffee for himself. He finished the coffee, disliking it, and then the glass of water that went with it. Lina didn't seem to think there was anything wrong with her ice cream. Mistler had not given up the intention to be nice to her, but such finer feelings were being shoved aside, because he was fighting wave after wave of nausea. He had always claimed, with justification, to have a stomach like a copper pot. He never suffered from seasickness, diarrhea, or constipation. The urge to throw up, the revolting act itself, was known to him only from the observation of others, particularly Peter Berry, who was susceptible in equal measure to indigestion and hangovers. Was the sour-tasting cup of coffee to blame, or was the liver he had on his brain saying hello? He had understood Bill Hurley to say that he could expect a truce of sorts. Was it over? Peter Berry usually asked for a Coke in similar circumstances. Mistler decided he might as well try one before it was too late. Amazingly, it worked. A medicinal property of that stuff—an account that the agency had twice failed to land, notwithstanding the personal effort he had made—or some basic medical principle at work, for instance that one dreadful taste will drive out another? He would have to inquire of the oncologist. For the moment, he was grateful to Peter for one concrete, even if small and unwittingly bestowed, benefaction. It would take a lot more to even the score, of that Mistler was quite sure.

Can I have another ice cream—chocolate and pistachio this time? Or do you think that would be piggy?

It was a relief to see that his victim was returning to her ingratiating and submissive form.

Not at all. You deserve it, after all that work taking mug shots of me and the long trot from the church to here.

I love your face. You look like that man, only your nose is shorter.

She pointed at Colleoni.

The Coke was not a perfect remedy. He replied: You mean I look just about as disagreeable.

In their sophomore year, Peter put off all work on the Victorian literature course they were both taking until the end of the reading period. A twenty-page paper on *Great Expectations*, which counted for more than the final examination, was due the next day. He hadn't written a line; worse yet, he had never read the book. Total despair. Not handing in the essay guaranteed a failing grade. Mistler had done his own paper on Pip—as an intolerable prig and snob. During the night, he composed its mirror image, discussing the innate qualities that were destined to make of Pip, unmistakably, an English gentleman. He avoided the question of whether an English gentleman isn't necessarily a snob, if not a prig. Both essays received an A-plus and the section man's illegible encomium. Peter was grateful. He was able to keep his John Harvard scholarship. Mistler didn't mention, and Peter hadn't seemed to notice, Mistler's struggle with the code of honor, drummed into him at boarding school, which equated what he had done with cheating. Something else went unmentioned, though perhaps not entirely undetected by Peter: Mistler's worry that Peter might be getting into trouble, overestimating his own facility and believing it the equal of Mistler's. Was that a danger lurking in their friendship, was he a bad influence on Peter? Ha! His influence! Two years later, in the empty interval between graduation from college and reporting for military duty, came the dismal news of Jeanie's pregnancy. Practically since the day she arrived at Radcliffe, Peter had been sleeping with her every other afternoon, unless she was having her period, in the bedroom he and Mistler shared in Eliot House. Those were afternoons Mistler spent at the Widener or in a boat on the river. The insemination could be traced to a particular Friday, when Mistler was in New York and Peter, having earlier that week bounced several checks off Harvard Square merchants, found himself unable to pay for the package of condoms he was accustomed to buying before each of Jeanie's visits, at the pharmacy on the corner of Boylston Street. Unable to convince Jeanie that her mouth was a sufficient receptacle, he attempted to exercise self-control. Discipline and resistance of pleasure were not Peter's strong suit, as Mistler subsequently had occasion to observe and point out to him.

Once more, panic and despair. She was a smart Jewish kid from the Bronx on the way to a *Vogue* internship in Paris. There wasn't a chance of the Berry parents allowing Peter to marry her. They were as long on family credentials and related principles as they were short of cash. Besides, Jeanie and Peter had already broken up, her berth on the Berry afternoons having been taken by a long-legged nymphomaniac from Cleveland. Mistler got in touch with Madame Portes, the one person he was sure would know what to do. She was in Paris; two days later she called back with the name of a doctor on East Eighty-sixth Street. It's really not for you? she asked. Very well, I won't ask again, but, if it is for you, be sure you are very kind to the girl. Now, and especially when it's over. Don't let her down. Mistler imparted this advice to Peter, along with cash for the doctor's fee, went with Peter and Jeanie to the appointment, and remained with Peter in the empty waiting room, reading one issue of *Life* after another. Then they took her in a taxi to the apartment of a girl already working for *Vogue*, so that she wouldn't have to return home to the Bronx until the next morning.

Mistler recalled the incident when he told Peter to retire. The reasons for forcing him out were solid; he had asked Voorhis to review them: Peter's working week and attention span had shrunk to one-half of what might have been acceptable in someone drawing a third of his salary. There could be no debate about that, but Peter was ready to argue that his capacity to reform—and inalienable rights as a cofounder of the firm—had been disregarded, and, of course, that Mistler was acting in bad faith, although he had been offered a two-year consultant's contract, one that he could perform from his farm in Dutchess County or wherever else he pleased, provided he was within the hypothetical reach of the telephone. In the last negotiating session, when Mistler was alone with him, the lawyers having withdrawn at Peter's request, Peter shifted his weight in the armchair, blew a fart, and told Mistler, I could accept it all, if you weren't still the prick who stops at nothing to get his way. That was when Mistler decided to add a flourish to the revenge he had settled on before. He rejected Peter's one remaining demand, that he be paid the difference between what would be the price of his shares if the agency were sold to some prowling buyer in the next five years, and the book value price he was actually receiving. That difference turned out to be a tidy sum, important even for a man who had become rich. Mistler calculated the precise amount during the lunch at which he made the deal with Omnium. He thought it was neat that no one would ever be able to show that he had been thinking of such a transaction at the time he finished off Peter.

Do you know your worst fault? Lina asked him. She was licking the spoon. He would have bet she was debating the wisdom of eating a third gelato.

Perhaps. What do you think it is?

You're only interested in yourself. You haven't paid any attention to me since we sat down here.

Really?

Really. And it's really bad. You know that you haven't asked me a single question about myself.

That's one of the many forms of my discretion. Besides, it's more amusing to figure things out without asking. I think I could tell you a lot.

Try!

Let's see. I will err on the side of the aforementioned Mistler discretion, and take the risk that you will think I am superficial. You are just under thirty, but because you have very good skin and don't seem to have had children, I could be off by a bit. You might be as old as thirty-five. Your speech is without accent or inflection. Nevertheless, I think you are a New Yorker. One of those superclean, tightly knit Italian neighborhoods in the boroughs? Sheepshead Bay? Somewhere at the outer limits of Queens or the North Bronx? Perhaps as far as Yonkers? I would think, though, that you've always lived somewhere near Manhattan. You've zipped in and out by subway. I have the picture before my eyes. In the subway train, a perfectly made girl with straight brown hair, a serious pale face, something terribly well scrubbed about her, as though she had just stepped out from the shower, blue jeans and a denim jacket, her backpack or camera bag behind her crossed legs so they can't be snatched. She sits between two fat ladies. No way a dirty old man like me can snuggle up to her and rub her elbow with his. He might stand in front of her, though, hanging onto a strap, and make knee contact.

Jeez, Thomas! I bet you've never taken the subway in your life. I bet you don't know what the fare is. You've been going to Woody Allen movies.

He had to keep talking. Otherwise, he would sink.

Totally wrong, he told her, although I confess I've lost track of what the fare is. That happened when the toll machines stopped taking quarters. My secretary buys tokens for me. But I'm a student of subway-car advertising. In my opinion, Preparation H ads belong in the Hall of Fame. And those sublime pidgin-Spanish cartoons about AIDS. Pure genius for drama and dialogue. If only Tennessee Williams had lived to read them.

He stopped and covered his mouth. It was unthinkable that he should rush into the toilet of a place such as this and puke. Perhaps he would be all right if he took deep breaths very slowly. Another Coke. He waved to the waiter and pointed at the empty glass. It was too difficult to reach for the handkerchief in the pocket of his trousers. He wiped the cold sweat from his forehead on his sleeves.

Is something wrong? You've turned green.

No—or rather yes. I think it's my new hay fever pills. I had better be quiet for a moment and drink that Coke.

She put her hand over his on the table. It was nice to feel the warmth. He imagined himself in bed, lying on his side, with her also on her side, pressing against him very tight. Or with Clara. To feel warm all over. The waiter returned with a Pepsi. No more Cokes. Mistler drank it and then ate the slice of lemon that had been floating in the glass. The effect was the same. Pepsi was only less well advertised than Coke, after all. Breathe in and out and think of something else.

You might have gone to the high school for music and art, he continued. And then photography courses at the School for Visual Arts. You became a photographer's studio assistant, possibly he was your teacher at the school, before you started freelancing. And, of course, you've had a long affair with a married man who wouldn't divorce. That broke up recently, just before Gansevoort, which is why you are drifting. Drifting sexually, I mean. Your ma and pa out there in Sheepshead Bay don't like that, but there must be some siblings who are married, who come to Sunday lunch and so forth with children and spouses. One of them lives in the neighborhood. How is that?

Not so good. I mean I like the story, but it's not about me.

Really?

Yeah, really.

All right. You tell me. If you want to.

It won't spoil your fun?

Promise! Don't pay attention to me, Lina. I'm feeling better. Let me sit here quietly and listen.

Point one—you're wrong about the boroughs. I'm from upstate New York. Ever heard of Oneida? It's west of Utica. Oneida was a famous free-love colony in the nineteenth century. There's the table silver factory there too.

That explains it!

What?

You. You're a daughter of Aphrodite.

Wrong again! I'm a daughter of Mr. and Mrs. Mahoney. My dad worked in sales for the silver factory, but he came from Rome. I mean Rome, New York. Just on the other side of Oneida, if you're driving from Utica.

You could have been a foundling. You mean your name isn't Verano?

It is. I married a guy called Luigi Verano. But my first boyfriend came from one of the colony families. I can tell you those guys know how to screw. It's in the genes. They just keep going and going and then start over again. Jeez!

Repeated erections are not uncommon among healthy adolescent boys. And where is he now—I mean Luigi?

In Milano. You got that right about being a studio assistant. I was his assistant in New York after I left school, only I went to NYU. They've got a good photography department. That was when my dad was still alive. I had to quit when he got sick. A couple of years later, he died.

I'm sorry. My father died when I was considerably older. He had been a great help to me.

My dad got cancer. It started on his intestine. The doctors thought they took all of it out when they operated, but it had spread to his liver. Then they tried to cut it out from his liver too. It was gross.

Ah!

Yeah, it really got to me, the stuff about that saint's liver.

I'm very sorry.

It's OK. You couldn't have known. My uncle is a priest in Utica. He said masses for my father just about every day. It meant a whole lot to my mom and to my dad too. I'm not religious like them, but Mom still goes to mass every morning. We were brought up to be good Catholics. Look at me now!

Because you are divorced?

Because of the way I live! By the way, I'm only separated from Luigi. He isn't in any hurry to get a divorce. I'm like an umbrella—I keep the broad he lives with off his back. Your friend Mr. Gansevoort thinks I can get a divorce in New York and just send Luigi the papers. He's even found a lawyer for me. If I ever save enough money to pay her, we'll see.

Good for Tony. He'll pay, I wouldn't worry about that. Do you mean he has asked you to marry him?

More or less—he's talked about it. I hate to tell you this, Thomas, but it really ticked me off the way you talked about religion inside the church. What kind of name is Mistler anyway? Are you Jewish?

I do have one Jewish great-grandmother, but I don't think that qualifies me. The name has a French origin, but my original Mistler ancestor came from England. But then, in the nineteenth century, a great-grandfather of mine married a Quaker from Philadelphia. I suppose you know that Quakers don't get baptized. They don't need to. They have a direct line to God. But she's the only Quaker in the family. It's all been downhill ever since, in terms of contact with the Almighty. I was baptized, and so was my son, Sam. Kicking and screaming.

So what's with you? What was all that stuff?

Nothing. I'm not a member of atheists anonymous. I talk too much. Too much rhetoric. Sometimes I like to hear myself talk. I didn't mean to upset you.

Sometimes! You sure did. Anyway, you're the one who drags us from one religious painting to another. All those crucifixions and martyrs. That's all you look at.

Because it happens to be what medieval and Renaissance painters painted—that was their great subject, like naked women washing their rear ends for the post-Impressionists. I look at all that torment and slaughter because of how they are painted, not for the content or the message. I hate the content and I hate the message. I think about how the Christian religion was hijacked, so that in churches love and forgiveness are crowded out by scene after scene of pain and all the ways men can hurt one another. I include in that Jesus Christ too, his wounds still open, sitting on his throne and judging sinners, sending them to concentration camps operated by Satan.

You're really disgusting.

Well, what kind of religion is it? We are told the church was founded on the rock and that rock was Peter. All right, Peter himself was crucified, though not so painfully as his Master. The church lives for the glory of the Son of God who was tortured and crucified to death, but it goes on to kill and torture. It's number one in that activity. Just think of totaling it up: the Crusades and wars of religion, expulsion of Jews from Spain and Portugal, conversions of heretics and Jews extracted on the rack and by fire, major contributions to the massacre of Indian populations all across the Americas! Not so long ago, in Europe, a cross with Jesus Christ on it stood at every crossroads. In churches, crucifixion after crucifixion. As I said, it was the one big subject for artists. I accept that. I like especially the northern crucifixions, where you find, swarming all around the cross, hardworking little men, incredibly concentrated on their task. Keen piglike eyes, red bonnets that cover their ears and are tied with a string under their sagging chins. You see every horrible wrinkle and wart. What are they up to? They are busy hammering nails into Jesus' feet! Every tool of an honest carpenter's trade is there, perfectly rendered, even ones like a saw or rusty pliers that you wouldn't think are immediately needed. One supposes that the men who served as the painters' models, or their fellow guild members, at one time or another really rolled up their sleeves and did equally grue-some things for the glory of God to some flesh-and-blood people right there, in the great square before the cathedral, under the supervision of the local bishop! Why not to one of their own neighbors? A guy who of his own free will commit-ted this or that crime against the Holy Ghost!

Thomas, the crucifixion was a sacrifice, a sacrifice God made for man.

So I was told at boarding school and before that in grammar school. It's a sacrifice I do not understand. I've also been told that it's normal that I can't, because the mystery surpasses human capacity for understanding. I should also tell you that I don't understand God's testing Abraham by asking him to kill his son Isaac. A poet I admire wrote that hell expresses God's supreme wisdom and love. I don't buy that either. What about your father's liver? How does it fit into the scheme of love and goodness?

Jesus God, Thomas, stop. I've had it. I want to go back to the hotel.

Right. I am very sorry. Do you want to walk?

Not if I can help it.

Another huge loop. The vaporetto threaded its way through the Arsenal. She wasn't too mad to hold his hand.

How long were you married to Luigi?

Three years. We got married when he decided to move to Milano so I could work there, you know, get a permit. He's a good egg. We might have been OK if we had stayed in New York, or if we hadn't had the kid.

The kid?

My daughter, Alma. She lives with him, I mean with his parents. He won't let me take her out of the country. I'd get arrested if I tried.

That's hard. How old is she?

Her eighth birthday was last week. She's a great kid. The trouble is she's forgotten almost all her English, and you know how I am with Italian! Maybe he'd let her live with me some of the time if I married the right guy.

I guess I was wrong about your age too.

Yeah, but don't tell. Tony thinks I'm twenty-eight. Most people think I'm under thirty. It's more like forty.

Does Tony know about Alma?

I've told him.

Marrying old Tony Gansevoort might not be such a bad idea. He has bags of money, you know.

Yuck. I'd rather marry you, even with all your talk.

Believe me, Tony's a safer bet. It could be that he's a nicer fellow too.

The nausea had settled as a bad taste in his mouth. When he spoke to her, he made a point of looking away. A cold breeze was blowing off the water. He was glad when she put her arms around him. It made very little difference who got on or off the boat and was able to see them. He remembered how, in the Gesuiti painting, above Saint Lawrence and the torturers, a mysterious lady wrapped in black stands on a pedestal that seems to grow out of an urn decorated with heads of lions. She holds in her hand a small statuette. It's an offering she has brought to the temple. Mistler felt he had become enveloped in a blackness like hers.

[VII]

He awakened because his bladder was full, and tried to hang on to the dream. It was no use. The lively complicated details, the action he thought he had mastered so completely, all of it went out of focus and became unrecognizable, like a flower bed after a frost in September. He extended his arm toward Lina. While they were getting undressed, he told her he was too tired to make love. He preferred that to the truth, which was that he wanted the sickness to recede, and hoped it might if he lay on his back very quietly, the covers pulled up to his chin.

It's OK, she replied. I'm beat too.

Then she added, Boy, that was some afternoon. You sure know how to make someone feel bad, really bring them down.

Once again, he said he was sorry. That was the truth. What had been the point of dragging her down with him into his misery if he was unwilling to let her know of what it was made? Those were the only words they spoke, but a little later she moved nearer and touched him. He didn't stop her; the caresses didn't distract him from keeping the nausea at bay, a project which needed his entire attention. Now, about to get up from bed, he passed his hand over his stomach. Judging by the flakes on his skin, she had made him come. Or had he had, miraculously, a wet dream he couldn't remember? One or the other must be the reason why he had slept so profoundly. No, Lina wasn't there. On her side, the sheet was cold. The blanket had been pulled back in place and smoothed. Mistler staggered to the bathroom, urinated, rinsed his mouth, and decided to lie down again. That was much better. With another hour of sleep the soreness in his legs and back and the bewildering feeling of nervousness might leave him too. For how long? That was another matter.

The windows of the bedroom were open, but the shutters muted the half-maritime, half-urban noise of the Grand Canal. Deep, unbelievable comfort of the huge empty bed, the blanket wrapped tight around Mistler's trunk. Desire for Lina: at first, like a half-formed caprice, then growing precise and insistent. He had missed the conscious experience of the climax to which she had brought him, the moment when her fingers would have been wet with sperm. Hot impulse turning into cold glue. She had given him pleasure by treating him like an object. Did her pleasure, assuming she had felt any, derive from his passivity, and her power over his body? But was it real passivity? Hadn't she jerked him off because she knew what he expected of her?

A whole lifetime ago, he wasn't yet forty—Lina's actual age, come to think of it—he traveled to Tokyo nearly every month, on business he had thought up that had come to seem important. In the end, it failed. He had wanted to bring Showa, the largest Japanese advertising agency, into a partnership with Mistler, Berry. Nearly always, he took the flight from New York that arrived in Tokyo in midafternoon. On one of his early trips, he was invited by the head of Showa to dinner at six-thirty, less than three hours after his plane was scheduled to land, an implausible hour for dinner that the Japanese considered standard and imposed, although in the circumstances it was quite impractical. The car ride from the airport could easily take three hours. Since his hosts knew when he was arriving, he didn't see what he would gain by protesting. At six-twenty, while he was frantically looking for the cuff links that had to be on some surface in the bathroom or the bedroom—but which one?—the telephone rang. Mr. Tadachi, the head of Showa, "and the other members," of whom there turned out to be four, were already in the lobby. They got into cars, made a brave start in the direction of Hibiya, and then crawled and stopped and crawled and stopped in the rush-hour traffic past the Ginza, which lay somewhere to the right, heading east, beyond the Imperial Palace, until at last they reached a warren of wooden one- and two-story buildings decorated with plastic versions of paper lanterns. The one before which the motorcade halted turned out to be a tempura restaurant, a branch of an ancient Osaka establishment. They took off the blue plush slippers that they had worn for the march down the corridor and, in their socks, filed into a private tatami room that had its own, as yet untenanted, counter for cooking. This was the real thing. Under the low table on which the food would be served there was no space into which foreign guests—and even Japanese diners not averse to a little cheating—might insert their legs, thus combining the appearance of tradition with modern comfort. Sitting cross-legged, therefore, but having shed his jacket and loosened his tie to attain the equally important appearance of informality, Mistler drank cup after cup of sake poured by a young woman, something more than a waitress but not quite an apprentice geisha, on her knees beside him, consumed a seemingly endless series of side dishes that continued to appear until the tempura chef bowed his way into the room, spared no unction assuring the mama-san kneeling next to Mr. Tadachi that the meal in progress was more refined than any he had previously eaten, and took care to keep the conversation with his host off any subject of importance. It was not the right moment to try to get down to business; the time for that, he had been taught, would come the next morning, at Showa's office. With increasing frequency, Mr. Tadachi smiled at Mistler, said, Just a minute please, and talked volubly with his acolytes in Japanese. Time-out for Mistler. He would wiggle his toes and work on the cramps in his legs. Certain key English words, slightly distorted, recurred in the Japanese conversation. Dividend, cash flow, major clients. Equivalents had to exist in the Japanese language. Were these crumbs that his future partners were leaving for his guidance, like Hansel and Gretel, or a show of contempt? Didn't they care what he might infer?

Pleading the need to call his New York office before colleagues he had left behind in that distant time zone were busy in meetings, Mistler refused the invitation to follow the tempura by a digestive stint at a nightclub. It didn't seem likely that whiskey-and-sodas and a couple of hours of necking with a relay team of bar hostesses would advance his business. He felt no nostalgia for memories they might revive of Wellesley girls and their silk stockings, and of the way they had of stopping your hand, but not before some progress had been made. A chauffeur drove him unaccompanied to the hotel, the other cars presumably on their way to the best that Ginza or Akasaka had to offer. By the time Mistler had made his telephone calls and undressed, he thought he could distinguish a separate ache in each of his bones and joints. He dialed the number of the hotel massage agency and asked for a masseuse. A young masseuse, he added, curious what the request would elicit.

Masseuse in fifteen minutes all right? inquired a singsong voice.

All right.

He dimmed the lights, set the knob on the night table for the tea dance music the hotel piped into rooms at that hour, and lay down on the bed. When he opened the door, it was to admit a middle-aged operative with two gold teeth. She disappeared into the bathroom, reappeared, arranged the pillows on his bed for the procedure, wrapped a towel around his midriff, and got to work on his shoulders. Astonishing, implacable fingers created their own heat.

Strong massage OK?

OK.

New question when she reached the small of his back: Double massage OK? Double price.

A groan of assent.

Just a minute please.

She spoke into the telephone.

Back to his body. The pressure became more intense and different. When she kneaded his buttocks, something—was it her elbow or the edge of the palm of her hand—thrust into the crack between them, driving straight, it seemed to him, at his anus. He felt the beginnings of an erection that was independent of his mind, certainly disconnected from the charms of this businesslike, short-legged lady. Farther down. Work on his thighs, particularly the inside. Her hand felt for his scrotum, examined it, and continued downward into regions of progressively smaller interest. The back of Mistler's knees, his calves, which she tormented, his toes. She snapped them one by one.

Feel good? Lie on back please.

The erection had become enormous. It peeked out from under the towel. She wagged her finger and, shaking her head, began the reverse journey up his leg to the land of the balls. A brush of her fingers here and there. She lifted the towel and examined the situation with a frown.

Long time not make love?

He shook his head. No. What would the double negative mean to her?

Special massage? Not tell anyone?

This time he nodded yes.

She masturbated him like no other woman, better than anything he had been able to manage even at school, when he would drop his homework, smear cream on his hands, and writhe on the dormitory bed. When he burst, she wiped him with Kleenex, and continued. At the end, she used her mouth. Having spat daintily into more tissues, she observed, Double come. Strong.

After she had cleaned him with a wet washcloth, she inquired: You stay Tokyo?

Yes.

When you want massage, you ask Matsumota. Remember?

I will.

That had to be her name and not the word for the operation. With exemplary efficiency, she remade his bed and transferred the towels to the bathroom. When all was in order, she handed him a hotel charge slip to sign, bowed, and shuffled out the door, in her hand the plastic bag in which she had brought her talcum powder and baby oil. Why had he recalled this scene, apparently so banal? What made it powerfully erotic, causing an erection of unaccustomed vigor? His feelings about Lina seemed to mirror the confusion he had felt then, as to what he had done and what had been done to him. In Tokyo as well he had been uncertain whether he was the actor or a prop. The Japanese lady had been under no obligation: all he had asked for was a massage. The rest was her invention. She must have liked playing with his tool, making the dumb rich stranger ejaculate, twice with hardly a pause, in her rough hands, and then in that dentist's nightmare of a mouth. That could have been a way to tell him who was boss, to degrade him. And the vast surge of his pleasure, was it from degrading her, from knowing that, without his having lifted a finger, a no-nonsense, middle-aged woman, surely older than he, who should have been at home cooking sticky rice for her husband, performed those services? Degrading her, and being degraded. By her. Wax in her hands. Wasn't that what he looked for in sex, the reason he wanted Lina so urgently? She would spread herself for him. With her own hands. Before he had asked.

He didn't bother to put on his bathrobe. Stroking himself, to remain powerful and swept upward like a boomerang, he strode to the door of the living room and thrust it open. Just as he would thrust himself into her, right there, while she bent into a U over the gueridon. But Lina wasn't in the armchair where she usually read or on the sofa. The room was empty. Mistler felt his erection turn into flannel. On the floor, where he couldn't miss it, was a sheet of hotel writing paper folded in two with "Mr. Mistler" on it underlined twice. He picked it up and read:

Goodbye, Thomas. I hoped our few days together would be sweet. A harmless adventure for both of us. When I met you at Mrs. Williams's dinner I thought you liked me, though you certainly stayed all cool and polite.

Now I realize that cool and polite is all you are willing to give, and you aren't all that polite. Not when the bully takes over and you start putting someone down like this afternoon. I was going to leave tomorrow afternoon anyway, to get on with the job in Paris, but I think I better go now. You will have an extra day to be alone with someone whose company you really enjoy—yourself! I know that's a bad old joke, but I can't resist it. You don't need to feel sorry for me, but if you get over being pissed and remember that you said you would help me get some work from your agency I will be really grateful. I'll even say a prayer for you. How about that?

Thanks for the clothes and all the nice meals.

That's all I guess. Have a nice time!

Lina

P.S. I don't think you really like women. I'm not even sure you like the sex. So what's with you?

The breeze off the canal was chilly. Shivering, Mistler closed the windows and went to the bedroom to get his bathrobe. He reread the letter, crumpled it, threw it into the wastebasket, and said out loud, because the silence in the room was intolerable, I didn't need this but I sure asked for it. Then he corrected himself. He hadn't asked Lina to barge in on him in Venice. The one time they met, he hadn't encouraged her. The business of wanting to photograph him was pure effrontery. It was she who deserved whatever she got. In fact, she did get exactly what she wanted: a stay in Venice in a fancy hotel and a promise of work for the agency. Her mistake was not to have left nicely. His mistake was not to have thrown her out in the first place. The good news, as she might have said, was that he need not see her again. There wouldn't be any overtures about having a drink or lunch in New York. The bad news was that the letter might be a feint and she wasn't leaving the next day. She was a snoop and knew about his plans. What if she was really booked on the same flight for Paris as he? She might show up at the airport with a "here I am, I've been naughty" smile, obliging him to choose between equally disagreeable alternatives: brushing her off and doing the right thing, and that meant upgrading her ticket, arranging for her to sit next to him, giving her a ride into town when they arrived. Who knows? She might want to go with him to his hotel.

There wasn't any reason to shave a second time before he went to dinner, but he did, and then finished reading the *Tribune* in the bathtub. The market was down and so were the shares of Omnium and the other listed advertising agencies. He hoped that trend would continue until the day when the exchange ratio of Mistler, Berry's shares for shares of Omnium was fixed, but not so sharply as to get out of the collar or for too long afterward, lest his troops grumble, regretting that they hadn't received payment in cash. That stocks go up and down is easy enough to observe, but people have trouble keeping it in mind. Mike Voorhis had told him the lawyers would have the documents ready for signature in another two weeks. Once the cat was out of the bag, he would need to talk to a lot of people. The staff at Mistler, Berry and Omnium, clients other than the few into whose ears he had already whispered, trade press, bankers, analysts. According to Voorhis, Jock Burns was planning a joint appearance with Mistler at a gala lunch to be held at the Plaza. Nausea, a weakness in his arms that was like being mugged—they didn't seem to diminish his mental agility. But to remain affable, even-tempered? That depended on not feeling rotten. The black cat would have to be let out of the bag, too, and properly introduced to the Mistler family. Perhaps he could get Sam to come to New York for the weekend directly after his own return to New York, using as a pretext the important, confidential business news about to become public. After all, someday it would be his money. Then he would tell him and Clara at the same time. At Crow Hill, if possible.

He got Lina's letter out of the wastebasket and reread it carefully. There was nothing in it to have gotten so hopped up about. Had he told her he was sick, she would have tried to comfort him. She might have even succeeded. The "adventure" had been degrading in bed and out, a point he didn't need his new prism to see. They had both asked for that. As for his not liking women or sex, that was an interesting observation. Perhaps her expectations were too high; perhaps she was right. She would have her pathetic agency assignments. He never went back on a promise; it was too bad she didn't realize that. On the other hand, where would she have learned the ins and outs of a gentleman's code of conduct? With Tony Gansevoort, you dope. What she hadn't asked for was the stuff in the Gesuiti. And then, in that dreadful café, he had upped the bidding unfairly, to the point of assaulting her. She would recover from it all; one keeps on recovering until the finish line is crossed, just as one cleans up after messy sex. Toilette completed, the body looks and smells as good as new. The psyche also perks up. Everything ends well, because everything ends, Madame Portes had remarked after a visit they made together to the hospital during his father's last depression. That assumes one wants things to end, he replied. She did not accept that. *Chéri*, she told him, your wishes are not *à l'ordre du jour*.

He had gotten only as far as Santa Maria del Giglio on his way to dinner when he felt the drizzle. Was it going to rain hard? A downpour after a series of such absolutely perfect days wouldn't surprise him. What was the weather forecast? He had not bothered to read *Il Gazzettino*. Regardless of what it said, there was absolutely no reason to risk getting soaked. The restaurant stayed open until all hours, and he had made a late reservation. In fact, he was pretty sure that the owner, Signor Nerone, would have already uncorked, and maybe even decanted, one of his good bottles of red wine in anticipation of Mistler's arrival. But Mistler didn't want to turn back for the sake of his umbrella. It would be an opening for the annoying concierge to relate once again how he had pleaded with *la signorina*—according to rules applied with speed one would wish for in-room service, Lina had been demoted to a younger age group or a lower social category—to allow him to call a water taxi for her, and how, rejecting his solicitations, she had disappeared into the *campo*, all alone, her suitcase rattling behind her on its little wheels. *Basta!* He turned up the collar of his blazer, crossed the bridge, and briefly followed Calle Larga 22 Marzo. Turning left, he passed the Fenice. Nerone's was twenty steps away, in Terrà degli Assassini, a small filled-in *rio* that ends at the canal linking the Bacino di San Marco to the Grand Canal, after the latter has made its vertiginous first turn. Inconvenient lovers, foreign merchants who carelessly show off the ducats in their purse, and, after this dinner he was so looking forward to and the heady wine, perhaps even Mr. Mistler—so many trussed-up bodies cast on nights such as this into the murky flow! No weights attached to their feet. Instead, thugs count on a lucky confluence of currents and tides to carry the dead man out of sight and out of mind past San Giorgio to the narrow beach at the Lido. With the Virgin's blessing, the corpse may even drift out to the gulf and the open sea, leaving behind Le Vignole and the obstacle course of islands and shallows in the lagoon. It was a passage that a living man might want to try, pushing off in a gondola or skiff, hunched over his oars, quite alone, surrounded by ooze and flights of startled birds. Or would one try the harder run, to the south?

Mistler looked in through the window. Nerone's was in reality a *vini*, the size of a diner on lower Tenth Avenue. For a weekday night, the crowd wasn't bad. Tables in two booths that were large enough for four diners had been set instead for two. The one next to the kitchen was where Signor Nerone and his assistant would have dinner after the last guests had been served. On the other table, a pitcher filled with red wine and the bottle from which the wine had been poured waited beside the starched white napkins and a basket of bread sticks. That must be Mistler's table. Too bad! One setting would have to go. Mistler walked in, waved in the direction of Signor Nerone, and sat down.

[VIII]

Back in the hotel, he calls Clara. She has decided, after all, to go to the Voorhis dinner, yes, this very evening. Really? That's very thoughtful. He wouldn't have dared to urge her, but Mike will be especially pleased. No, they won't mind her coming alone—far from it! Mike has worked hard for the agency, especially the last few months. They'll be thrilled that she hasn't begged off, even though Mistler is away. Yes, of course he is particularly pleased too. He knows she is doing it for him, and not for Mike or Ellen Voorhis. Can't she tell he is pleased? Who else will be there? No idea, but there will certainly be other people. Oh, some partner from the law firm who does work for the agency, perhaps Schwartz, the tax man, and his gynecologist wife, country neighbors from Garrison, that sort of thing. Sam hasn't telephoned? That is annoying. Absolutely, she needn't read any special meaning into it. No, there is always a meaning? Perhaps he is just busy and, anyway, she knows he doesn't like to chat on the telephone. Antisocial behavior? That's a bit strong, but if that's what it is, it's directed at the world at large, not at her. Ha! Ha! The girl? Which one, Monique or the kid? Certainly, it's sometimes awkward to talk to him knowing that Monique is in the room, but one might as well get used to it. They're getting married! She's right, there is nothing we can do about it. Well, then call him at the office. If he doesn't answer his phone, the thing to do is to leave a message asking him to call, or to get him at home, when Monique is at the clinic. Yes, that does mean calling after five in the afternoon New York time. Oh, he telephones Sam whenever there is something he wants to say, Monique doesn't bother him. That's right, or the kid, Linda. No, that doesn't mean he is so superior, just less sensitive. No, he hadn't had dinner with people. Isn't it their rule not to know people in Venice, or to make dates with other Americans passing through? He had dinner alone, at Nerone's, rather late. It's amazing how Nerone puts up with those hours. Right, he went there late because he took a nap and didn't feel like getting out of bed. Yes, and then he felt like going out. Oh, the usual crowd. Two tables of locals plus French and American old-timers. In fact, a French couple she knows was there. He didn't sit down with them; they said hello on their way out, and sat down with him. Yes, it was just what he wanted. Simonnet. Arnaud Simonnet, the banker, and the wife who has the designer look. Yolande, her name is Yolande, but Simonnet calls her Yo. Right, in the "I am still a young thing" line; when they used to see them, it must have been Cardin. Right, boxy in the shoulders and showing quite a bit of leg. This evening? She wore a pantsuit and leather. Straps, big belt, vest—decidedly not S&M, more like Hermès. No, they didn't say much, mostly talk about French politics, all the latest horrors about Mitterrand, that kind of stuff. They didn't eat with him, they had already finished dinner. Just drank some of his wine. It was just as well; he might not have made it to the hotel if he had finished the bottle himself. No plans to meet them again. No, he doesn't. To see Yolande? What a bizarre idea! Certainly, Simonnet would like to be friends, it's he, Mistler, who is antisocial. That's right, just like Sam. He will call her next evening. Yes, before six her time.

When had she become so leaden and boring? The question was rhetorical, one of many Mistler put to himself to blow off steam. For that purpose, no answer was required. When he occasionally did consider the matter seriously, he was far from sure that in this particular respect she had changed very much. Her slowness, the habit of taking in whatever he had said and then going over it at least twice to make sure she had it right, those endless questions—when you say you will call me tomorrow evening, you do mean evening New York time, not when it's evening in Timbuktu? and all its cognates— were they new? Once upon a time, this particular tic, really it was nothing more than that, had amused him; he teased her about it. The change had been in him. The ordinary form it assumed was impatience. That was why, even when he was on his best behavior, as he had just been, what might start out as apparent solicitude quickly showed as condescension, the filter that transformed her pleas for reassurance into the unbearable nagging of a confused, dissatisfied wife. Worse than that. Humiliated. Clara obedient and brought to heel when he confronted her about Peter Berry. Each party had received equal value in degradation, the currency of the bargain: a nicely balanced transaction. She didn't believe for a minute that he had forgiven or forgotten—any more than she had. Probably, she was convinced that the deal was present in his mind every time he thought of her, certainly each time they fucked. That would be how she put it to herself; he had been taken aback, but also titillated, when she used that word right away, refer- ring to their first copulation, and, ever since, possibly because she had sensed his excitement, she stuck to it. Would it be a further humiliation if he assured her, before it all ended, that she was in error, that his recollection of the wrong, and of the hatred, was only intermittent, like marsh fever?

Simonnet and Yolande had surprised him. That they should greet him in the restaurant was probably unavoidable, although, in their place, considering that they had given no sign of recognition on the vaporetto, he mightn't have bothered; it was easy enough to walk out of a place like that, eyes fixed on the door, although the noisy leave they were taking of Signor Nerone had distracted him from his breaded pork chop, and he happened to look up. Chalk that up to stupidity, parading as politeness. But was there any need to ask, after he had risen ponderously to shake their hands, whether they might join him, and then to accept his slow-to-come offer of a glass of wine? It wasn't the first time Mistler had cursed the gregari-ousness that afflicts tourists, the compulsion, upon meeting an acquaintance on foreign soil, to progress straightaway to a familiarity not authorized by prior dealings. In Simonnet's case, the need—or was it training?—to cultivate business con-tacts at every opportunity, even when the circumstances would seem particularly unpropitious, must have played a part. But the gaffe that followed was excessive. What need had they to inform him that they had seen him earlier in the day on that vaporetto, to comment on the absence at dinner of his charm-ing young companion? It contradicted the only benign expla-nation of their failure to greet him then: the old-fashioned rule that you do not acknowledge the presence of a man accompanied by a woman who is not his wife or a member of his family unless he acknowledges your presence first. And then to ask—it was Yolande's question—whether, if they all remained in Venice until Sunday, which was what the Simonnets intended to do, they would have the pleasure of meeting her. He said no with such brutal finality that it would have been reasonable for them to flee at that moment. Instead, to his further surprise, he found himself being treated by Yolande to a smile blending indulgence with worldly wisdom. Patting Simonnet on the forearm, as if he too deserved her sympathy, she observed, Ah, your young friend had to leave Venice before the weekend! A working girl, with a career. They're all in such a hurry—they can't take the time to be happy, not even in this divine place.

Mistler didn't reply.

Apparently determined to pursue her thought to the end, although he could not see a connection, she added, And that poor Elisabeth Portes! Such a tragedy! To die so young. We haven't seen you since she disappeared. You were so close. Her sister, Mireille Leroux, the widow of Professor Leroux, the cardiologist, of course you know her too, she speaks of you with great admiration.

This was a third surprise, particularly unwelcome. He could recall Simonnet's saying, at the end of some business meeting, that he knew the sister of Madame Portes, and had learned from her that Mistler was her friend, and the one time he had dined at their apartment with Clara, Yolande had made him wince when she uttered the name of Madame Portes. Having no intention to discuss his most intimate concerns with these business acquaintances, he had limited his reply to an all-purpose grunt.

According to Mireille, it was a terrible illness.

Yes.

Mireille said you visited Elisabeth regularly. So few impor-

tant men would do that—all the way from New York! Had
you known her for a very long time?

Friend of Mother's.

Of course, many of her musician friends were also remarkably attentive. She had done so much for music, and artists do
have time for friendship. Not like busy men, such as you and
Arnaud. What a wasted, unfulfilled life! Married immediately
after convent school to a disagreeable friend of her father's
who was old enough to be her father himself—and he died
right away, without leaving her a cent. It wasn't as though
there had been *un polichinelle dans le tiroir*, I think you call it
a shotgun marriage in American. Never remarried, no family
at all, except poor Mireille and her son. You know that boy
now lives in Brazil. Strictly *entre nous*, having him so far away
is breaking Mireille's heart. Living alone is difficult for
women when they get older. Especially in a case like Elisabeth
Portes's. And then to die in such total solitude! Don't you think
that on the deathbed only the family counts?

Simonnet interrupted: Hadn't Elisabeth Portes had a long
involvement with some man who wouldn't or couldn't marry
her?

I don't know, admitted Yolande. I think there were many
men. Probably entirely inappropriate.

Madame Leroux must have considered her sister's affair
with Mistler's father very inappropriate indeed, a disgraceful
concubinage, something she considered a skeleton in the family's closet. Otherwise she wouldn't have been so discreet.
These busybodies weren't likely to have forgotten a name as
unusual as Mistler, had she mentioned it, and, if by a miracle
they had, it would have come back while they guzzled his
Barolo and gossiped about a dead woman they had never

known. Mistler remembered Madame Leroux with distaste. During those dreadful weeks, she had worked to make sure that her sister wouldn't, in a moment of weakness or folly, neglect family duty and leave her money to the lover's son. It might have been an anxiety of long standing. Whenever he found himself alone with her, for instance in the corridor outside the sickroom, while the nurses, behind the curtained-off door, were busy with some unmentionable task, Madame Leroux talked about inflation, which had eaten up her widow's pension, and the bleak view the *notaire* took of her finances. She was obliged to spend principal. Of course, Elisabeth was free to do as she wished with her fortune, *cher* Monsieur, but if she gave the matter even a little thought, she would realize that it was within her power to make her nephew independent. What a relief that would be for his mother! The boy was engaged to a girl of good family, but without a cent. When they married and had children there was literally nothing they could be sure of except her own tiny, shrinking fortune. Mistler supposed—in truth, it was very clear—that she hoped to appeal to his sense of delicacy, if not of family duty, that had perhaps atrophied in her sister owing to her unconventional way of life. In such case he might, during the many hours he spent tête-à-tête with Madame Portes, forbear from persuading her to disinherit her own flesh and blood. Or, if she had already formed an evil intention, at the last moment prevent her from committing such a crime! Being entrusted with a task that should have fallen to the parish priest would have amused Mistler in other circumstances. He wondered whether she dared to hope that Mistler might, if worst came to worst, renounce the inheritance in favor of the natural heir.

The possibility that she might also be badgering Madame

Portes about money horrified Mistler. With infinite precautions, he begged her to assure Madame Leroux that she need not fear for her son's expectations.

Madame Portes laughed—the timbre of her voice and the thrilling cascade of her laughter had not changed. Ah, the Leroux boy! If I didn't have *l'esprit de famille,* I would indeed leave it all to you. Your father was so generous, and whatever I didn't spend right away was invested very wisely. First he made me a happy woman, Thomas, and then he made me rich. You know that when all his trouble came he refused to let me help.

There was no need, Tante Elisabeth. He had more than enough to repay the losses.

I should leave to you at least the jewelry. It's all presents from him. That little prune the Leroux boy wants to marry will never wear it. It will be sold. *L'esprit de famille!* You are the son I wanted, the son that he and I should have had. Thomas, your success, it isn't all on the surface?

In my life?

That too. But in your business?

Tante Elisabeth, nobody lives grandly anymore, but I may be richer than Father ever was. And the rest? It's all right, *sans histoires.* Anyway, I'm not like Father. When I wake up in the morning, I feel good. What lies ahead during the day or the week doesn't seem to matter.

He was like that too, she said, but only on the outside. Then she slipped off her finger the ring with the enormous oval sapphire and closed his hand around it.

He gave it to me after the first visit we made to you at school. You haven't forgotten? Don't argue, I want you to have it.

Mistler looked across the table. The Simonnets had not

disappeared. He would remember them with distaste as well. What a useful, as well as curious, coincidence, though, that they should have made him think of the sapphire! Clara had never seen it. As soon as he returned to New York, he would get it out of the bank safe, and, when Sam came, he would present it, over lunch at the club if it wasn't too late, in the cracked red leather stud box that had belonged to his father, just as he had put it away. Some explanation would be needed, enough to make clear that it was not just the price of that amazing stone that mattered. His son could then decide whether and when to give it to Monique.

Could Madame Simonnet be waiting for an answer? Simonnet had finished his glass of wine. Perhaps he wanted to have it refilled. Neither husband nor wife was stirring. The silence was grotesque.

How is the bank? Mistler asked. I suppose we do business with you.

Not nearly enough. I would like an opportunity to talk to you about it.

Nowadays, I leave all that to other people. Speak to the head of our treasury operations in London. Meanwhile, we mustn't bore Yolande by talking shop, and we must let Nerone lock up.

It had stopped raining. Yolande said they were at the Monaco—his hotel was on the way—they could walk back together. This couple stuck to you like Elmer's glue.

I have sprained my ankle quite badly, he replied. It would be best if I limped home alone.

His bed newly made and turned down, the bathroom in order, fresh flowers on the coffee table in the sitting room. On RAI Tre, some sort of fifties movie. Fat Louisiana state troopers hassling in fluent Italian a kid with a crew cut and a comb sticking out of his shirt pocket. The cruiser's motor is running, there is noise of static on the radio, the emergency light goes round and round. Mistler thinks he has seen the movie but can't recall its name or plot or who is playing the kid. He could stick with it to improve his Italian, but what's the point; he is leaving in two days. Clicking the remote control, he finds CNN weather, two Italian politicians talking their heads off, a film in German of the sort Sam used to call intense, and another with a girl taking off her clothes in front of a man who doesn't pay attention and goes on with his meal. Why bother to watch TV? There is a VCR hooked up to the set. Mistler wishes he had gotten a videocassette. He opens the minibar. The ice tray is empty. It would be less sordid to call the hall porter and have him send up a real bottle of whiskey, San Pellegrino, and a bucket of ice. But drinking in his room alone will depress him. He might as well brush his teeth, take two sleeping pills, and hope for the best. Why not check out the hotel bar? Or, across the Accademia Bridge, the nightclub with an Arab name. He has passed by it countless times. God knows what kind of clientele. You can bet that it's still open and doing a good business. Just in case, he does brush his teeth and goes downstairs. Sorry, sir. The bar closed at eleven. To hell with it. There is no need to cross over to the other bank for a bar that's louche, although in another genre. He heads for the Rialto, walks past it. The place is just as he remembers. By golly, the rain having stopped, there are even some men at the tables outside. It's not an establishment where Mistler would normally choose to be seen; certainly not alone, unaccompanied by a woman. Why give that any thought? He won't hang out on the terrace; that's too much. The light inside is bright white, like in old-time cheap Italian joints in New York. There are several empty tables. He sits down and waves his hand to attract the attention of the waiter.

A double scotch with soda and only one lump of ice. It washes away the ache streaking across his forehead, just like diving into the furrowed, quirky water of the bay years ago, when Sam still spent parts of the summer vacation with them, and, after the week in the city and the ride in the car fighting sleep and reading his pile of papers, he would arrive at Crow Hill to a noisy welcome. That is when he feels a hand on his shoulder and hears a familiar voice: *Siete voi qui, Ser Tomasso?* He recognizes it at once. Barney Fine. No one else would have said that. It doesn't matter that the last time they met was God knows when—three, or five years ago?

He turns around. Holy Moses, there he is, grinning, excessively tanned, thinner, and, because he stoops, no longer so prodigiously tall. Quite bald on top, with long wisps of white hair that seem to grow from behind his ears, dressed in the same chinos he wore in Harvard Yard, year after year, autumn, winter, and spring, ending a good inch above the dirty sneakers he still has on his feet. That's where the sartorial identity ends. This evening Barney sports a navy-blue wool gondolier's blouse instead of the brown tweed jacket worn so threadbare that it was edged with suede inside the buttonholes, as well as at the elbows and the ends of the sleeves. Mistler has to admit the garment is becoming.

Aren't you ashamed to be caught here by your old buddy? What if the word gets around? Man, you will be on the front page of the *Village Voice*! You're in for a major problem with Clara. She'll sue for annulment!

If it's the price of seeing you, that too will be bearable. But what are you doing here, I mean in Venice? I recall getting a card, with Xania as your permanent address. Why aren't you there? This must be the best season for Crete.

It's so perfect you wouldn't believe. I still have the house. You know what? It was built by a Venetian merchant, when this place colonized us. Hey, you remember my friend Leo?

I do. He was at the agency—the graphic artist. Left after a short while.

Right on! We met at the agency. We've been partners ever since, and now he's fucked me. For a Greek goatherd, for Christ's sake, the kind of guy that, in the old days, used to lay you, take your two dollars, and didn't give a shit whether you came or not. He's got him living in my house! All of a sudden, the house and the whole frigging island seemed crowded. I came here to wait it out. Either it's a passing fancy for Leo, or I'll have to turn them both out.

Wouldn't that be tricky?

With the Greek, yes, you bet your sweet fanny. Remember Bobby Crane? He had a house on the port, three doors away from ours, and a goatherd of his own, only that pisser was really a waiter in the taverna. Anyway, one day Bobby realized that he'd stolen his mother's candlesticks and so he ran to the police. The boy went to jail all right, but when he had served his term he came back and chopped Bobby's head off with a meat cleaver he borrowed at the same taverna! What do you think of that?

Deplorable!

Leo had better keep that cautionary tale alive in his *cabeza*. The pity of it is that all the silver in the house is mine. I'm staying here on the Zattere, with Bunny Cutler.

Is that a he or a she?

A she. You know her. She was at Radcliffe, in our class.

I don't.

You've forgotten. Why not? I don't think I knew more than twenty people in my class, and I bet I've forgotten all but five. She lived with Feretti for years, until he died. I'm sure you knew him. Your mother certainly did.

You mean Enrico Feretti, the composer? Yes, Mother knew him. I never did. That part of her life went on in the winter in New York, when I was at school, and then at college and in the navy. Very few of her artiste friends showed up at Crow Hill.

That's too bad. You've missed a remarkable personage, and I am not speaking only of his genius. He was the last great Italian monster. Screwed whatever walked, swam, or crawled— any member of the animal kingdom, even women. Insanely rich, of course. He entertained beautifully. Sodom and Gomorrah in full, special action under one roof. Believe me, pure bliss. Fags and dykes flying in for weekend parties from London and Paris. Too bad for Bunny. He left everything to a boy from Costa Rica, including the most beautiful palazzo in Venice that had always been in his family. In the end, he adopted the bambino, so the kid now calls himself the Marchese Lopez-Feretti! But Bunny manages all right. Hey, come to lunch!

Do you think I'll fit in?

We'll see. When Enrico was still around, I would have lent you a gold chain and some leather. Now that's optional.

It's a deal. Meanwhile, can you get that ephebe to bring us some scotch? And, just for a change, lots of ice?

Barney knows his way around, Mistler thinks. Good poet, too. The overlay of Allen Ginsberg is so thin it doesn't get on your nerves. Ah, enough ice cubes to sink the *Titanic*. What was left of Mistler's headache is gone. Now it's just bile swishing around. Time to light a cigar. In such matters, Mistler is free of pretension; although in one of the pockets of his blazer there should be a box of wooden matches, he makes do with the Bic he bought for a thousand lire. Even after a second blast of flame, the damn thing won't draw, perhaps because it's moist. Delicately, Mistler reams the cut end with the blade of his penknife. The improvement in that quarter is immediate. Mistler wishes he could say the same for his stomach. Down, Rover! Once upon a time, not so long ago that he can't remember, the body was a source of simpleminded contentment. Later, the trick was to keep it at arm's length in good condition, to serve as a sort of tailor's dummy. Now it's hell. A few months of this stuff can be endured. But if it were an eternity? Forget it.

Where is the chaste and beautiful Clara? You two haven't split?

No.

Good! In that case, I get the picture: she sleeps off the day's tourism in the *letto matrimoniale* while gay blade Mistler *fa un piccolo giro*. Shame on you, Thomas! You should begin to act your age.

It's becoming obvious to Mistler that Barney and Peter Berry are in touch. Barney has heard every single detail and is now sticking in the knife. What a fool he was not to have questioned Clara himself. He should have made her tell him and then show, over and over, how they had done it, each one of those things he has never asked for because she's his wife. Ha! What's the use? He is stirring cold ashes. Images that drove him wild for thirty years—excitement, desire—they are as dead as the past itself. All he feels is guilty embarrassment, no different from turning the pages of a dirty magazine at the hotel newsstand while the porter is getting your luggage.

Meanwhile, Barney is giggling. Can that Jewish s.o.b. read one's mind? Mistler wonders. Why is he looking at me that way?

Actually, she is in New York doing good deeds on my behalf, he informs Barney. At this hour she should be dining with the agency's lawyer and his not-so-chaste wife.

That's unreal! You've really changed. Gung-ho Mistler taking a bachelor vacation!

A prompt onset of prudence: if he tells Barney the truth, Barney will phone Peter. Might as well hold a press conference and call off the deal with Omnium! Therefore, he answers: This is the tail end of a business trip to Milan, Barney, that's all. I took a couple of days off to pay my respects to some Titians. Apropos of nothing, I don't think I've seen you since that party you gave in someone's apartment on East End Avenue, near where my parents used to live.

That's because I've hardly been back. I do business, though, with your London office.

You do keep up with the old gang in New York? You and Peter Berry used to be great pals.

We were, in the *Advocate* days and at the agency, and later, too, while he and Jill were still married. Until she left and he rented my house for the following August. I had just finished redoing it from A to Z and needed to cover some of the cost. Man, they really wrecked it. It was like a demolition party gone wild. The neighbors couldn't believe it. Some crazy scene. After a week, even the boy who looked after the garden couldn't take it and quit. When we got back, everything Leo

had planted was burnt to the ground. Peter didn't even bother
to water. Like an idiot, because it was him, I hadn't asked for a
security deposit. Anyway, it wouldn't have been enough. He
refused to pay for the damage. I haven't spoken to that shit-
head since.

No kidding!

Leo said it served me right, you should only rent to queers.
Fortunately, enough of them like it in Xania!

That's an awful story. I'm not on very good terms with Peter
either. Do you know that I've never been to Crete? Clara took
Sam to Knossos, during one of those vacations when I thought
there were things at the agency that only I could do. I've
always wanted to go. Daedalus and Icarus! King Minos's
palace! The Minotaur! All my favorite stories. I would have
liked to see your house too.

It's not too late. For you I might even bend my rent-only-
to-queers rule—that's if Leo ever gets the goatherd out of
my bed.

Barney, let's have another round of these fabulous drinks.

Sip sip. Mistler hears another man's mellifluous voice. The
man is confessing to Barney: It's too late for Xania, old pal, too
late for everything, because, very soon, I will be dead. I told
you a little lie a moment ago. There was no business meeting
in Milan. I came here to be alone. Nobody else knows, not
Clara, not Sam. Just the lawyer Clara's having dinner with and
the doctors. So you must promise to keep the secret until next
week. That's when I plan to stop lying to her and Sam. You see,
you are really the first person who isn't in the death business
to find out. It's made me feel better to tell it—even if it's a
little unfair—I mean unfair to you.

You poor bastard! Cancer?

The silent kind. Just sits there and grows. It's gobbling up my liver. The doctors think it could be linked to a virus I caught when I was with the fleet off Taiwan. Chinese who have had a certain kind of hepatitis tend to get that cancer. So far nobody has suggested it's the booze!

Shouldn't you lay off anyway?

Why? For the sake of a few more good days? That's not enough reason to change a lifelong habit. Probably, I have enough time left to do the few things I need to do. Come to think of it, perhaps it's quite fair that you and I should be talking about how my life ends. You are one of the authors of the adult part of it. I don't think I would have gone into advertising if you hadn't talked about your job. Just think! Without you, I might have become a big-game hunter or an insurance salesman.

Or a writer. That's what everybody expected. Including me. Remember, the plan was to write copy, so that you wouldn't have to take money out of the family piggy bank. You weren't supposed to become a fucking mogul!

I passed a turd. The novel I wrote was bad. You thought so too. If you didn't, you never bothered to tell me. Besides, I had the feeling I had scraped the bottom of the barrel. There was nothing else to tell. You are different.

I've kept writing.

You haven't just kept at it—you've managed to move ahead. I liked your last volume a lot. I even wrote to you to say so, and I meant it. You can use verse now to say exactly what you mean, without veils, without ricochets from the work of others.

Thomas, you don't know what's in the barrel until you go back for more and scrape hard. I think you stopped because you got absorbed in something different that you didn't want to interrupt. Right away, at the old place, when I got you that job, you were good at it. Man, you had a lucky streak, and you just kept winning. That was all right, so far as it went. Later something changed. When the three of you started your own shop, it was as though you had lost yourself in it. A writer has to hold back some space for himself, so he can see and do things his way. Launch an attack on the unknowable!

What shit.

I beg your pardon. With you, when you went into the business, it had to be all or nothing. From where I sit, when I think who you might have been, it was ass backward. Sure, you've got nothing to regret. You're the great hero of advertising. The playboy of the postmodern world. I'm a respectable minor poet and a hack copywriter who depends on guys like you to make a living on the fringe. By the way, I hope you can arrange for my deal with Mistler, Berry to continue after you're gone. So who's done it right, assuming one has any choice in the matter?

Who knows? In my case, I'd almost say I had no way out, not at that time. I began to want to start my own business right after my father disgraced himself. It's absurd when I look back on it now, but I had the feeling—really quite irresistible— that I had to make up for it. The interesting question is: To whom? Had I told Father what I was up to, he would have said I was nuts. Quite mad! But I thought—I was convinced— that I had to put on a show of great competence. I didn't believe I could do it with another novel, I'm sure the idea never occurred to me. There was a simpler solution. If Mr. Mistler Senior no longer rules the roost on Wall Street, young Mistler can be king on Madison Avenue. It was as simple as that and as stupid.

I never heard of anything happening to your father.

Apart from Wall Street types, few people did. You know that my grandfather was the head of the investment bank. Our name is still on it. He was quite a fellow, a legend of sorts, having actually made money all the way through the crash. It wasn't exactly easy to follow him into the firm. Nevertheless, that's what my father did, right after college. When the war came, he was old enough to stay out with complete honor, but that doesn't seem to have crossed his mind. He pulled all the right strings, Grandfather was able to pull some strings as well, since Colonel Stimson had been his lawyer, the commission came through, and in due course Father got recruited to do special services work in France. He spoke French perfectly and was monotonously brave. I talk about him this way because I loved him with my whole heart. Meanwhile, Grandfather minded the store. Even after the war, Father stayed involved with the spooks. According to people who know about these matters, from time to time he did some very fine things. Between you and me, he found his mysterious voyages to Europe, that Mother couldn't question, convenient for certain personal reasons. At the same time, of course, he took back his place at the bank. Since Grandfather was very old by then, that meant running the firm. It really was another world. Father went through a depression right at the end of the war—perhaps it was more like a nervous breakdown— and these depressions recurred in a milder form, but no one seemed to think that disqualified him from working *pro patria* or at the bank. The greatest possible discretion was the rule. He was, as it turned out, a very good banker. Nothing like Grandfather, but the bank grew and was remarkably profitable, and Father cut a great figure on Wall Street and in New

York. All of that was completely genuine, because he was the finest man alive and thought very clearly. In fact, he thought so clearly he foresaw the monetary turmoil that began at the end of the Eisenhower years. Therefore, he zigged—I mean he took some extraordinary positions with the bank's capital without consulting with his partners, which was not unusual, because Grandfather and he weren't in the habit of asking anybody's leave when they knew they were right. Unfortunately, almost immediately after that he went into one of his depressions, and when the time came to zag, his mind wasn't clear. He did nothing, his partners were so appalled that they did nothing, and an enormous amount of money was lost. The bank's capital, clients' accounts, the whole shitload. Thereupon, Father recovered and put back everybody's money. That meant selling his collections and every other piece of property he had, except, of course, the apartment and Crow Hill, which were in his and Mother's joint names, cleaning out the last cent of cash that wasn't tied up in trust, borrowing against the money that was to come to him when Grandmother died. By the way, she did just that almost right away, from shame, as my mother liked to explain. He hadn't done anything illegal, you understand. It was just a piece of monstrous mismanagement by a man who ought to have known he shouldn't be out on the high wire. It brought the bank to the edge of ruin. That's all. He took limited partner status at the firm right away, in theory to save appearances, in reality because the partners didn't know what to do with him except turn each of his remaining days into hell. Then he began to have little strokes. In spite of all this stuff I could have done just what you say—I could have kept my private space and squeezed out a novel or two. Instead, I succumbed to a fit of genetic puritanism. So that's one story I will never get to write.

Man, somebody will!

Why not you? You used to write prose. All those sensitive stories about good Jewish boys with problems about their identity. Then you discovered the Horatian ode! Thank God, that passed too.

Mistler, you've always been a prick!

How interesting. The last time I saw Peter that's what he said. One plus one makes right? No? Hey, don't take this personally, it's a pure coincidence, but I must puke. Got to find the john *prestissimo*. Don't go away. I should feel better afterward.

Turkish toilet. Just as well, because it's not only vomit, but also diarrhea of an unnerving color. Mistler thinks of the day, a lifetime ago, when he ran crying to his nurse, and she said, Don't worry, it's the beets you had for dinner. He sacrifices to hygiene the linen handkerchief in the pocket of his pants and, when that isn't enough, the square of Charvet silk from the breast pocket of his blazer.

Barney is still there, both hands around the glass, staring into it. He looks neglected and old. Perhaps Mistler should yield to the temptation to offer him the money to get a bridge for where his lower incisors used to be. How many copies could his *Ribald Muse* have sold? Four thousand? It seems you can chew on one side only and stay in perfect health. What's the use of Mistler's carefully tended muscles and agile body, serene face, and luxuriant head of hair kept in perfect trim by the best of barbers? They're on their way to the compost heap. One can't help thinking it's a raw deal. Nonetheless, the well-bred face remains serene. He sits down. The waiter is sulking nearby.

Barney, do ask your pal for more scotch.

He does. In Mistler's opinion, his own Italian is better. For instance, he uses the subjunctive with gusto. Why hasn't that poet learned it?

Putting his hands on Mistler's, Barney addresses him: Man, it's wild to ask you this, but here goes. Are you scared? I mean to thaw, resolve, and all that shit?

Not yet, so long as I think that there is nothing more to it. I have two wishes: One, I'd like to get out painlessly before I become too weak or too fuzzy in the head to stop these well-meaning fellows with Hippocratic oaths and funny initials after their names from showing me the marvels of modern medicine. Two, I'd like to avoid accounting for my sins. You remember that poem of Baudelaire's where he talks about the anatomical drawing of a skeleton, spade in his bony hand, turning over clods of earth forever and ever? I wouldn't like anything like that to happen.

Amen! You can say that again, baby. Can you imagine the shit I'd be in!

The first wish, that's another matter. You'd think that, as a member of the patrician class, I would have faithful slaves Primus and Secundus at my Rhode Island villa to run the hot bath and open the vein in the hollow of my elbow. Well, I don't. I don't know of any agency that gets temporary help like that for you. It will have to be self-service. Exactly what I have always disliked the most. The last few days, I've been paying particular attention to the giant-size black plastic bags in the trash bins in Venice. Do you suppose the big ones are better than the ones you use in the kitchen?

It's tough to do, man. You know Eddie Laker? He'd gone blind in one eye, could barely see out of the other, he was down to a hundred pounds, he had the pills, and he couldn't bring himself to take them. I said to Carl, Why don't you put a pillow over his face and just leave it there? He said it's Eddie's decision. Maybe he was right. Could be that every moment of consciousness is better than the big Niente.

Right now, I don't think so. If you remember it, ask me in three or four months.

Have you thought what this garbage bag bit will do to Clara? Or your son? Jesus, Thomas!

What do you want me to say? Frankly, I haven't been able to give Clara much thought. There are reasons for it, in addition to my being a prick. My son, Sam, whom you don't know, is a good guy. We haven't gotten together much in the last few years, because he has been living on the West Coast. He's with a nice woman now, who already has a child. They plan to get married. I figure if she has one child already, there isn't any reason why she wouldn't have another. I would like to see that. A new, fresh, sweet baby. It wouldn't have to be for long— just long enough to have it in my memory. Then there are things—physical objects—I am sorry to leave. A car Father gave me when I was in college. I never cracked it up. It's in good condition, I use it when I'm in the country, and I guess Clara will sell it to the gas station owner who will resell it to some jerk. A big beech at the end of the front lawn in Crow Hill. You might take the view that the tree and I will be eventually reunited. In my family we get married on that lawn and buried under it, so when I melt and dissolve I'll be feeding its roots.

And that's it?

Not quite. I have a sort of distant cousin in New York, who must be all of twenty-two. A countercyclical child: completely pretty and well groomed, down to her adorable toenails, which she paints with clear varnish. I saw them last summer but it sticks in the mind. We had lunch, and she wore sandals with high heels and no stockings. I like looking at her. No Barney, there is nothing more to it because there can't be more.

Thomas! Have you looked at your watch? I've got no idea when I can get a vaporetto to go back to the Giudecca at this hour of the night.

Go. I'll settle up. If you get tired of waiting for the vaporetto, you can sleep in my living room, at the hotel. I'll tell the concierge to let you in.

You will come to lunch at Bunny's tomorrow? You are going to like her. It's the sixth house to the right of Sant' Eufemia. Tall Gothic windows. Two o'clock?

If I remember anything of this evening, I'll be there.

[IX]

The Rector is dressed in a white robe, a short black cape over his shoulders, like nothing that has been seen at morning chapel before. Besides, it's not even morning; it is either the afternoon study period, or an assembly before the last football game of the season. The team is in the front pews, wearing their helmets. Mistler has been benched, because of the knee that still gives him trouble. He sits directly behind the fullback, Peabody, who hasn't washed and smells like a turd. Mistler can tell how the other guys are noticing it too. Kendall nudges his neighbor on the right—Mistler can't see who it is and doesn't recognize the number on his back—to make him move so he can get away from Peabody, but Peabody doesn't like that and wiggles his butt until he is even closer to Kendall. You are allowed to leave the chapel if you feel real sick, and Mistler thinks that perhaps he should, since the smell is making him faint, but it's too late; the Rector has begun his sermon.

Your nature is brutish, he intones, opaque to the light of God. Therefore, to receive God, you must be pierced by grace, just as the hands and feet of Jesus were pierced by nails, and his chest pierced by the spear of the centurion.

Is that right? Mistler desperately tries to remember, the

passage going around and around in his head, with words
missing. Was it the centurion or one of the Roman soldiers?
His head is unclear, because of the smell, but it doesn't matter.
He tastes something like vinegar tendered on a sponge.

Flagellants, monks in the coldness of ice, prostrate on stone,
chains, winter nights, smell, flesh mortified and wounded,
man consumed by suffering to let the soul awaken to the grace
of the Lord. The Lord's torment is repeated each time man sins
by oblivion, smell, swinish degradation of the flesh. Thomas
Mistler I have my eye on you, your pride will be broken, until
kingdom come and his will is done, one world without end.
The evil in you was born of greater evil, you are rivers and
streams flowing away from the sea. You will induce and
deduce these truths from the Word.

The Word of God continues, although the Rector has
climbed onto the altar table to lead the team in the school
cheer, while the lion of St. Mark's School roars like a waterfall
because the team has rushed him. Peabody is the first to reach
the beast, and that isn't right. He tackles the lion, hitting just
where Mistler hurts terribly. The Rector harangues Peabody.
It's a mistake; he means to address Mistler, in a language that
must be Italian. If it were Latin, Mistler would understand.
Each year he is first in Latin. He recognizes the words, *Non ti
piange ancora*, but not the meaning. Besides, the altar table has
changed: it is now a big square, like the *campo* in which stands
Santi Giovanni e Paolo, that has nothing to do with the table
at school. Through the ache, he realizes distantly that he has
been dreaming, but the dream isn't finished, it starts again,
da capo, with variations he knows he is inventing himself,
although, with his entire soul, he wants the dream to end. He
reaches for his glass of water, drains it, would like some more,

but won't leave the bed. Oh, he feels very bad. It is not, in fact, necessary to get up. A whole bottle of mineral water is right there on the night table, behind the telephone. He swallows two Valiums, not to sleep, only against loneliness and fear. What was Kendall doing in the chapel? He had been expelled the previous year, after Mistler twisted his knee in the third quarter of the Andover game. But this was the weekend when they played at home, the weekend when Father came to visit and brought with him Tante Elisabeth.

He knew his father would drive up in the Citroën, which was glamorously long and black, with front-wheel drive and a way of raising its rear end like a camel when it got going. Father, Mother, and he had toured in it on the way from Paris to Antibes, for a whole week, the summer before, and then, after two days, his father returned to Paris because he had business there. The car got shipped to New York; his mother didn't like it. Ordinarily, Father would have had lunch before the game with the Rector, his classmate at the school, but he seemed to have arrived at the last minute, with just enough time to shake Mistler's hand.

We're going to Boston for dinner, he announced. I have spoken to the Rector. You may spend the night. Meet me at the car after the game.

The Citroën was a cinch to find. In the passenger seat there was a woman he didn't recognize. Father and she were both smiling and waving. When Mistler waved back, his father rolled down the window and told him to put his bag in the trunk and get into the backseat.

You threw two fine passes, he said. I am proud of you. This is Madame Portes, my closest friend. I have particularly wanted her to meet you. Please call her Tante Elisabeth.

Hello, Thomas. I am so very glad to see you.

Vivien Leigh, his favorite actress: that's how Madame Portes sounded, English and not at all French. Her hair was curly, like Vivien Leigh's; it was almost red, and she wore it longer, it seemed to him, than other ladies. When she turned to face him he saw that she was so beautiful she could be a movie star, and young, probably not much older than Mrs. King, the wife of the new chemistry master. He didn't know Mrs. King's age, but when you saw her in a group of masters' wives, you thought she could be their daughter. Madame Portes wore a green pointed hat with a red feather. She made him think of a lady in a tapestry, leaving for a hunt, a bird of prey on her wrist.

She spoke to him again: Tommy has told me a great deal about you. That's why I am not at all surprised that you are such a good player or that you are almost as tall as he is.

He mumbled in reply something that must have suggested it was better to leave him alone. Afterward, his father and Madame Portes spoke nonstop in French, which he understood but didn't like to speak, for good reason: his father always corrected him, even though he spoke better than his mother, whose mistakes he seemed not to notice. The conversation was about their friends in Paris, and plans for his father's visit, which was to be before Christmas. Mistler lost interest and began to concentrate on his father's driving. It was particularly erratic. Most of the time he drove quite slowly. The bursts of speed came unexpectedly, often just as the traffic thickened. When they reached the three-lane highway, he took possession of the middle lane as though he were at the wheel of an ambulance. It might have been the effect this extraordinary car was having on him or some sort of joke, a way of showing everybody he could do as he liked. Madame Portes's calm was extraordinary too. Perhaps she talked so much that she paid no attention. Mistler's mother had ordered his father to stop the car and let her out at the side of the road in less provoking circumstances.

When they got to the hotel, Mistler's father said, We'll let Tante Elisabeth have a little rest in her room. She must need it after the way I drove. It's my wretched nerves. You put your things away and then come to see me. I have champagne waiting. Then Tante Elisabeth will join us for a glass and we'll go down to dinner. I bet you are starved.

The door to the suite was open. His father called out, telling him to make himself at home, that he'd be out soon. Mistler went into the living room and stood at the window. Below, lights in the Public Gardens twinkled like candles. When his father appeared, Mistler saw that he had changed into one of those dark blue double-breasted suits Sulka made for him in Paris. They hugged his body. Even so, he always wore them with a vest. Perhaps because of that, when his coat was unbuttoned, he appeared even more massive than he was in reality. If his face had not been so gentle and shy, he might have imparted a sense of menace. His father fussed with the bottle he drew from a bucket on a tray with three glasses, made the cork pop, and poured a glass for Thomas and himself.

Don't tell Dr. Endicott about this. He might laugh, but then he might not.

Yes, Father.

You see, when he and I were your age, Grandfather would come up for games, and he was not averse to giving us a little wine and we were not averse to drinking. Ha! Ha! But the Rector has gotten rather straitlaced with the years. It's a pity. One hopes that won't happen. Go ahead, have another one, if the waiter is stuffy I may not be able to let you drink at the table.

Mistler waited. This was only one of his father's prefatory anecdotes that served to delay getting to the point. He made fun of them quite regularly himself.

Of course, I haven't asked you to come here so we could talk about the Rector. I have something important to say to you. You are almost seventeen, Thomas, and very grown up. This last summer, when we talked about Karenin, I was struck when you said you liked him. You see, it's easy to like Vronsky, he is such a dashing fellow, and he does everything you expect such a fellow to do: he seduces Anna, loves her, gets bored, feels ashamed, goes off to war to get killed. Karenin is much more difficult. He has those big ears and he is pompous. Social and professional considerations count more for him than they should. By the way, that's where he and I resemble each other. All his passion is cold and sticky: he is unattractive even when he tries to keep Anna. Gets no credit for being good. But you said you could like him, because he was really trying. That's a very grown-up response, to sympathize with an unattractive man who is in an impossible situation. A man who doesn't know how to be different, who is decent but in a rut. We had another conversation, on the beach at Antibes. Remember, we talked about *Tender Is the Night.* You said you could see why Dick Diver didn't leave Nicole. I am not a character in a novel, but, if that helps, perhaps you can pretend for a moment that I am. I think you've already figured out what I want to tell you: I love Elisabeth—I have loved her ever since we met in France, during the war, when she was almost one year younger than you are now, and I don't intend to give her up. I know I can't.

Then you're going to leave Mother!

That's just the point, I won't leave.

Why don't you, if you love Tante Elisabeth? You and Mother don't get along at all. When you are together, it's horrible to be with you.

That can't be true always.

Most of the time. It makes me sick. I wouldn't care if you left. I could spend time with you and time with Mother separately, instead of watching you pretend there is nothing the matter.

I've talked to your mother about it. Not about Elisabeth, although I think she knows there is somebody, but about how we are bad for each other, and maybe for you. She has told me she will never let me leave. I can't do it against her will. She doesn't deserve it. And think what it would do to your grandparents!

They'd get mad. It wouldn't be the first time.

Thomas, there isn't any legal way it can be done. I can't get divorced in New York. I have no reason. Your mother hasn't given me legal cause. You can't divorce a woman just because she doesn't love you or you don't love her. And I can't go to Reno or one of those places and pretend I live there in order to get a Nevada divorce. The firm would go to pieces. Anyway, I've been told the divorce wouldn't stick, not if your mother didn't agree. I would be a bigamist when I married Elisabeth.

And you really love her?

Only her—and you. When I am with her, I am a happy man.

Then why don't you just live with her! There is that brownstone on Ninetieth Street you like so much, with a garage for the cars. I could have an apartment on the top floor to use when I am with you.

I've thought of that too, though I hadn't figured in how nice it would be to have a garage! It can't be done, Thomas. There would be a scandal. I would have to step down as the head of the bank. It's my duty to run it. Elisabeth agrees. Besides, she isn't sure she wants to live in New York.

Then leave the bank and live in Paris. You like it there.

Thomas, these are things Elisabeth and I have talked about over and over. Believe me! I am a little shocked that you find it so easy to think I should leave Mother and give up the bank, but I am more grateful than shocked. The way you feel will make it easier. You see, Elisabeth and I have decided we will live together, but discreetly. In Paris, and when she comes here to visit. She has just got an apartment in New York. I don't have to hide from your mother all that much. It's enough if we don't embarrass her.

I could never live like that.

I hope you will never have to. Make very sure of yourself and the woman you marry. Look, there are two things we need to talk about: One is obviously Elisabeth and me. I have not told you about her until today because you seemed too young and because I wanted you to see her before I told you, to realize how wonderful she is at the same time you found out. Now that's done. The other is also very important. I want you and her to become real friends. More than friends. You see, I'm putting together the two best things in my life. She will be good to you whenever you need her. You can trust her—always—when I'm no longer here. You don't need to pull a long face. I don't intend to check out anytime soon. Don't ever say I told you, but you should know that she saved me from getting caught by the Germans, just before the invasion. The way things were, that meant rather more than saving my life.

When she comes down, look for a little red thread in her lapel if she is wearing a jacket. She wouldn't put it on a dress. It's the Legion of Honor. She is probably the only woman alive to have received it as a military honor for something she did when she was still a schoolgirl.

What was it?

Something very dangerous that took as much brains as courage. She doesn't like it to be mentioned, but someday she may tell you herself. Please accept things as they are going to be. If you can get to love her that will make up for many things she has missed. I know I am doing my duty, but if you look at what I am doing from another angle, then I am selfish and weak. Like Vronsky, but without charm. And she is giving up her life.

How can you let her do that, Father?

I have told you, I love her. She loves me.

That was pretty good advice his father had given him. He might have added something about not having children unless one knew one's own character and had reached a satisfactory conclusion about it as well. One wondered what he would have thought of Clara, or of Mistler's having stayed married to her, or Clara's staying with him. Tante Elisabeth hadn't been fooled for one moment, since the first meal she had with him and Clara in New York, just before they became engaged. What a pity that he was too busy becoming a superman to understand what she attempted to tell him, so delicately, so beautifully. She was very sad; she had hardly had time to learn again how to put one foot in front of the other after his father's death. Later, he had nothing, not even his father's cockeyed explanations about the bank and New York divorce law, to justify the way he lived. On the other hand, he had no Elisabeth

Portes to love and be loved by. From the time Sam went away to school, there was nothing but *passades*, more or less tawdry, to weigh against reliable conjugal copulation on demand, Clara's superior performance as the wife of the chairman, and the principle of avoiding anything that interfered with his work, with his passion for the crushing exercise of power, for having his own way. Poor man: Father hadn't even had his way with Mother in bed. If appearances could be trusted, Mistler's conception had been immaculate. He was sure of one thing. If Clara had carried on like Mother, he wouldn't have just divorced. He would have broken her in two. It was curious that Sam had never spoken up, either for her, for both his parents, or for himself. Not even for the principle of sanity. That was, of course, Mistler's fault, not Sam's. Even with the war hero stuff, his Croix de Guerre, Distinguished Service Medal, and depressions, Father had been relatively approachable, and always gentle. Imagine trying to speak to Mistler on a subject he didn't want to hear about!

Was there anything to be gained from presenting his own case to Sam before the end of the play? The Magician bowing and scraping, apologizing that he lacks this means or that. Perhaps it would set Mistler free, but was that worth the risk of making Sam squirm yet another time? Was that unavoidable? One thing seemed clear: he couldn't let Sam grade his students' papers, fuss about whatever other university chores he had in mind, and then take off for Lake Victoria before coming back East. But, then, even if he could be made to squeeze in a visit to his father before the Rockies—doubtful, considering his basic mulishness unless he was told the truth—could Mistler spring the news on him the moment he walked in the door, or over lunch at the club, while he handed over Elisabeth's ring! And suppose Sam, as foreseen, wanted to bring Monique and the kid? Sure, it would be tempting to say he mustn't, it's the wrong time. But how would he feel once he was told? He might need to have near him someone he could hang on to who wasn't dying and wasn't his mother. Someone to creep into bed with at night. And it might, in the end, be easier to have Monique and Linda in New York or Crow Hill—to hell with Venice, Umbria, and wherever it is you can start shooting grouse in Scotland. Receive them on home ground. Let the medical bulletin become incidental music. If they were in Crow Hill, the kid would play on the beach or Mistler would take her out sailing. Pretend she is Sam's, even if she is a brat. There is no guarantee that one's own grand-children would be any better. Would Clara be up to it? She might never have a better chance to get on some sort of civilized terms with Monique. In all likelihood she would botch it: Why should one family visit, however dramatic the circumstances, do the work of two decades on the couch with Dr. Freud? But it could be her way out as well.

Should he call or write? The prospect of making a telephone call, from New York or Venice, was monstrous. Hello, hello, this is Dad. Everything's fine? Good. Incidentally, about coming home, here is the news, I'm dying. No, not this very minute, you don't need to rush to close my eyes, but in less than six months. Thought you might want to drop in while I'm still up and about! Right! If it's convenient.

There wasn't all that much to be said for writing either. The telephone had become the way they stayed in touch, and it was just as well. Over the years, his writing had come to conform to the "Mistler's Rules" he had imposed on offices from Thailand to Norway: Write to convince. Don't let your reader escape. If you can't make your point in one sentence, you haven't thought it through. Never ask a question unless it is specific and can be answered yes or no. (Example: Will you deliver my sofa on Monday morning?) Save time—when you receive a letter, reply in the margin, make a copy for the file, and return the original to the sender. When Mistler did write to Sam, it was usually because he felt called upon to get on his high horse—a need that had disappeared now that Sam was earning a halfway decent living and had also received outright quite a lot of the money that had been held for him in trust. Then the style was at its purest. For instance:

Memorandum to Sam, Subject: Spending habits. As your trustee I have, once more, transferred to the Donald Duck Bank X thousand dollars to cover the overdraft of dollars Y, notice of which has reached me. In the hope of avoiding the inconvenience of receiving another such notice in the immediate future, I ask that you oblige me by estimating your quarterly requirements. I will arrange to fund them. There is little point in saying that you don't need family money if living frugally in California means writing rubber checks. The Donald Duck Bank doesn't like it, and neither do I. I regret to advise that as your trustee I have no right to pay off the mortgage on Monique's house. I will be pleased, however, to invade trust principal and distribute to you a reasonable sum to enable you to purchase a house for yourself. Who lives with you in your house is very much your own affair. And, to forestall any sort of protest: Please understand that these are not mere technicalities, or evidence of any lack of desire on my part to make Monique comfortable and happy. Grandfather's trust does allow me to distribute income to you. Undistributed income, of which there is a lot because you don't want me to pay it to you, is added to principal. I may only invade the principal and distribute it to you in case of emergencies involving your health or to assist you in establishing yourself, for instance through the purchase of a residence.

He would sign, as though no other formula existed, "love Dad." Would it have been better to turn over the task of sending these missives to the family lawyer? Oddly, perversely, he thought that would put a still greater distance between him and his son. Should he have petitioned the court to have himself replaced as trustee? By the State Street Bank? By Uncle Abthorp, who would surely have refused?

This would be different. He would creep toward the subject that terrified him most—the silence dividing him from his son—on cat's feet. Sam, he might write, I have a sort of conviction that everything I so very much want to say while my mind is still unclouded, and while there is time for you to ask questions, you have already thought about over and over, and know the painful answers. But how can I be sure? It would be awful if I were wrong and, in our fumbling, constrained way, we lost this chance. I was grateful that you did not become hostile toward me as an adolescent, that you did not become a rebel when almost all your contemporaries seemed to. Alas, I shudder to think how clumsy and destructive I would have been face-to-face with overt rejection, and what I would have doubtless called, to your face, loutish behavior. But my heart broke (pardon the bathos, it's not the last time I will be guilty of it) when I saw how you had walled yourself off. Not only from Mom and me; one might have expected that and, had one been unselfish, perhaps rejoiced! From everything. From effort and pleasure, success and failure, adventure. Sex, too. At least, that's what I imagined, and it made me grieve. Knowing me as an indifferent husband, cold, and lacking in tenderness, you may find it droll that I cannot conceive of happiness except with a woman. I thought I saw you traveling farther and farther along a road at the end of which gaped, as though in an allegory, a cave surrounded by jagged rocks and dark yews. Within it, the figure of Negation: skeletal, half naked, hung with cobwebs. And so, when you decided to move to Palo Alto, to work there, to live so differently and far away from me, I was shamefully glad. I didn't need to have your sadness and what I feared would be your failure before my eyes. Oh, I would think about you and worry, and blame myself, but from a distance.

Le pire est toujours certain. Your grandfather was fond of that expression; he used it quite a lot. Tante Elisabeth must have taught it to him. For that reason, I like it too, but it isn't always true that everything will go badly. Your changed, new life, for instance. Your happiness. Your having become now the man I had hoped you would be when you were a baby and then a little boy, before you were hurt. Hurt by me. Was it learning how good your work could be or having found Monique that was the cure? Perhaps one wouldn't have been possible without the other. I doubt you could have let her love you if you hadn't healed.

Ah Sam, do you remember when we still played tennis together, before you decided that my serve was a murderous insult you would never again suffer? You announced that to me, just about the time when we waited to hear whether you had got the first job at the university. We had spent so many hours, conversations going around in dismal circles, waiting for the news, waiting. Because I knew how much the news mattered to you, the suspense was like the bird at Prometheus's liver.

Here Mistler stops himself. For God's sake, find another simile.

You got the news on Monday, hours after I had left for the city. Your mother called to tell me. Of course, with the difference in time zones, even though they called you first thing their morning—it was lunchtime at Crow Hill. You left immediately to catch the plane in Hartford and flew off to Alaska on the trip you had planned. And I did not hear from you at all, not for weeks, not until you called to ask that I transfer money to the account you had opened in Palo Alto. Just like that: the fact that you had gotten what you wanted, that you had succeeded where I most wanted you to succeed, became a subject that had passed by, never to be mentioned between us.

Then I decided that I must harden my heart against you. Dad, are you angry at me? you asked some months later. I replied that, of course, I wasn't, how could I be mad at my only son, and so forth. I didn't lie to you. I didn't tell you though that, in the meantime, I had realized that your love for me and my love for you were not commensurate. Of course, that's how it must be, it's the natural order. Good training, as they used to say in my day in the navy. Perhaps learning that I was alone with my love and hope is standing me in good stead now. But it seemed to me then that what was broken in me could not be mended any better than what I broke in you.

I have been beating about the bush. Until you no longer

allowed it, I forced my will on you, all along the line. I tormented you until at last you went on strike. Torment by water: you can't be that cold, you owe me another ten laps, and please stick to the crawl, what do you mean it's too rough for the dinghy, you won't win the cup if you don't practice, you know you can win. Family tradition: your great-grandfather, your grandfather, and I played on the school team, how can you refuse to try out? Comparison with me: I am not tired, sleepy, thirsty, hungry, cold, or hot. Why are you? If there were a Judge before whom I was going, a psychostasia, as in the great Torcello mosaic, with angels and devils on each side of the scales in which souls are weighed, he might find these were paltry, venial sins. The sin no judge can remit, least of all I, is how I forced your poor little body. Oh, it was all so much for your good, so much according to Dr. Spock and the medical fools I hired and paid, and you screamed with colic, but you were in my huge hands that nothing could stop, not when a job needed to be done. It is a memory I sank in the dankest well of my mind, where it remained submerged until the day your balsa-wood airplane knocked to the ground your great-grandmother's yellow Ming bowl. In rage, I broke the toy, while you cried Daddy, Daddy, Daddy. You couldn't believe that I would do such a thing.

Wrapped in the covers, his arms around the pillow, Mistler found that he too was crying. Can there be greater pain than remembrance of past sorrow in present misery? It did not seem so to Mistler. Fatigue, the pills he had taken, all that booze: like the dream of Dr. Endicott before it, his letter to Sam receded formless into painful distance. He could no longer manage his thoughts.

When he awakened, the room was very bright. He must have opened the shutters before going to bed to let in more air. He staggered to the window in the living room and looked out over the Grand Canal. Such a huge hangover! Measured against it, the dome of the Salute was like the head of a pin. According to his watch, it was a couple of minutes short of noon. The ringing of bells on every side of the hotel began almost at once, stopped, then started again, one church taking up where another had finished. To his surprise, Mistler held down his breakfast. In delay there lies no plenty. He put on the sofa, where they would be in plain view so he would not forget them, the faxes the waiter had brought with the tray, chose the small format of notepaper in the desk drawer, and sat down to write:

Do not wait to come home until August, dearest Sam, I implore you. Although I could not bring myself to say so over the telephone, there is a reason for haste. About two weeks ago, the doctors discovered that I have a lethal cancer. It doesn't make sense to try to remove it or treat it. Not to worry! I am not uncomfortable, and I am not likely to be for some months. Unfortunately, one cannot count on such things staying on schedule, and I would very much prefer that we see each other while I look and feel like the self to which we are accustomed.

I count on you to bring Monique and Linda, if Monique can possibly get away. Mom will be nice to them, I guarantee it, and I would be especially happy to have Linda run around in Crow Hill. Don't worry about Mom. Your own relations with her are likely to improve, if you let them, with me out of the way. You know that she has been unhappy as a wife for a long time. My immense joy when you drew closer to me necessarily made her resentful; of you as well as me, and of Monique, although poor Monique has nothing to do with our complications, and is, indeed, quite the sort of young woman Mom normally likes. By the way, if there is time, there are mistakes I have made I hope to talk to you about. I don't remember exactly what Dr. Johnson said about how a man's knowing that he will be hanged concentrates his mind, but I can assure you it's very true!

Since I will send this letter by courier, it should reach you the day I return to New York from Venice. Mom doesn't realize that I am sick. Please do not speak to her about it until I call to say that she already knows.

Well, that was that. There was tomato juice in the mini-fridge. He mixed a small quantity of it with gin. Some things could still be counted on. If a man such as he, *integer vitae scelerisque purus,* accustomed to pleasure, has an ugly death, need it be said that he has not had a happy life? For the moment, Mistler inclined to think the opposite. The stuff about not knowing until nightfall whether the day had been beautiful was clever twaddle. You took the day hour by hour and a life day by day. Why should the final passage be all that counts?

He lit a cigar, noted that it drew well and didn't make him sick, and sat down on the sofa to read the faxes. The first was from Clara, dictated to his secretary. She had tried to reach him after they hung up but was told he could not be disturbed. Thank God I remembered to tell the concierge I wouldn't take calls before I went out the second time! She would have been calling all night, would be on the telephone right now. The point was to remind him to buy and bring with him twelve clear sherbet cups to take the place of the ones that had been broken. Why not? He would get champagne glasses as well. One never knows when having another dozen will come in handy. The second was from Voorhis. Omnium's stock was down some more. The analyst at the investment bank advising Omnium was worried about its volatility. He foresaw a further drop as soon as the transaction was announced. Thereupon, Jock Burns called Voorhis and interrupted him at dinner to ask for a postponement of the transaction—a matter of weeks— to give the stock price a chance to firm up. How was he to answer? Mistler felt his face turn red and reached for the telephone. Voorhis should have rejected this piece of insolence out of hand; since he hadn't, Mistler would do it himself. A little past six in the morning in New York. It would do Jock a world of good to get a wake-up call from him. But his anger faded as he was dialing the number. Why not call instead poor Voorhis at a more reasonable hour and ask him to tell Jock that if that was how Jock and his advisers felt, he, Mistler, might also need time to reconsider the attractiveness of the deal. The likely result would be panic at Omnium, apologies, and everything being put back on schedule. Otherwise, the crab inside him might have the last word. It didn't matter. The agency was bound to be sold, anyway, though perhaps for less money than he had hoped.

He looked at his watch. The lunch at the house of Barney's friend—her name had gone out of his head—certainly wasn't before two. If he didn't dawdle in the bath, he would be only slightly late.

[X]

ON THE VAPORETTO that crosses from the Zattere to the Giudecca a girl with hair that's naturally red and a man who hasn't shaved are embracing. He has her lean against the metal wall, next to the entrance to the passenger cabin, his tongue in so deep he must be cleaning her tonsils. Mistler's view of the proceedings is excellent. He has his own back against the partition that encloses the bridge. Since he hasn't bothered to buy a ticket, he avoids eye contact with the *marinaio*. The distance is so short to the next stop that the *marinaio* isn't going to fetch his ticket collector equipment from the bridge. Probably Mistler is safe. It's a game, like any other. Mistler likes to play games if there are no rules. He moves just a little bit to the side, to have a better view of the couple's faces. More than ever, it's clear to him that fucking is the force that drives the world. What other reason is there for these skirts that stop just below the crotch, exposing thighs that beg for the palm to caress them inside, sandals with platform soles and drunken high heels that recall paintings of Venetian whores, bare midriffs and belly buttons, mascara, earlobes pierced by multiple earrings that promise obscene submission? He is out of that world. All the same, staring openly at the girl, he whistles, without Lina's dead-on accuracy but well enough, *bella figlia del'amore.* The man with stubble on his cheeks and a small stud in his nostril Mistler has just taken in is too busy squeezing the girl's rear end to notice, but the girl hasn't missed a beat. She gives Mistler a little wink. If Mistler knew the address of a high-class brothel he would rush there directly instead of looking for that imbecile Barney. The illogic of it all doesn't escape him. With very little effort he could have kept Lina around, until he got back to New York and Clara took over. It's just that he is burning.

That damn Barney never could get anything right. Or Mistler has forgotten how many houses from the church he was to count. Gothic windows. The fifth or sixth house. That's all to the good, but the names next to the buzzers are Italian and mean nothing to Mistler except for one, of uncertain origin, which is the name of a diva Mistler recalls having heard in something or other one hundred years ago. That cannot be the name of Barney's pal. The house beyond has a glass door. Through it one sees a courtyard of unexpected beauty. Bravo Barney! No dice; a brass plate informs Mistler that this is the entrance to archives the very existence of which he has hitherto ignored. On a side door, however, in addition to assorted Fabri-Vinci and Vinci-Fabri, he sees, next to a buzzer, the discreet clue: Piano Nobile. This must be it. He pushes it with his thumb. A noise to raise the dead ensues. No answer. Press again. Still no answer, but the door lock clicks open. *Piano nobile*, therefore one flight up. But of course! There, on the landing, stands Barney, looking like hell. He never went to bed or he slept in his clothes. Although Mistler is practically dead, and therefore less inclined than in the old days to guide his fellows toward self-improvement, he might, after lunch, tell him that one really feels better, whatever the circumstances, if one has brushed one's teeth, shaved, and put on something clean. Anything: even a T-shirt that says "Up Mine!" Mistler has never seen such a T-shirt, and he wonders why.

Holy shit, Thomas! I can't believe it.

I hope that you and your hostess did expect me! If you forgot, don't worry. My lunch canteen is next door. Why don't I invite you there?

Don't be silly. Bunny's all excited about seeing you. I just never thought you'd make it out of bed. You're the guy who's supposed to be dying, remember? But let me tell you, the leftover carrion—it's me. Hey, Bunny, he's here! Thomas! Big as ever and twice as natural!

He leads Mistler through a vestibule into the *salotto,* which gives on the canal. The light is colorless and cruel, because this bank is now in the shade. Mistler knows the view well, but has never seen it from above the Fondamenta. A Greek cruise ship is tied up on the other side. Next to it some sort of car ferry. The big room itself is on the squalid side: straight-back chairs upholstered with old velvet cheek by jowl with Holiday Inn Scandinavian loungers, a sagging sofa, a coffee table covered with last week's *Herald Tribunes* and a couple of leather armchairs. The antique carpet has tears in it that are signs of abuse. On the striped purple-and-yellow wall covering hang pell-mell portraits of men wearing red hats that come down over their ears, to make clear they are doges, and a couple of paintings of overweight goddesses gamboling in groups. Probably second-rate nineteenth-century copies that haven't yet made their way to one of the specialized dealers on the other side of San Marco. Also a large, drippy, violet artifact that looks like an Yves Klein but probably isn't. In this case, the inauthenticity is a plus so far as Mistler is concerned. Why spend money on stuff that any lout with a can of paint can make with the same effect? Aha, before the window is a table set for four.

From a room on the right he hears first high heels clicking on Venetian tiles and then the voice—throaty, mysterious, about to reveal the holiest of secrets.

Thomas, I can hardly believe it! Imagine Barney running into you! Or was it the other way around?

What reason would Barney have to play such a joke? The name Cutler has come back to Mistler. He is certain he doesn't know anyone, man or woman, called Bunny Cutler. But the voice! There cannot be any question about whose voice it is.

She has entered the room. Sadly heavier, and yet, if whatever miracle had allowed the skin to retain its ivory color had also preserved its smoothness, one would have said her face was unchanged: measured and tranquil features that have not thickened, startlingly large and wide-set eyes, and heavy hair. Pallas Athena! The hair had been like pale gold—long, touching her shoulders, parted in the middle and loose. It flew behind her in the wind, like a heraldic pennant, when she rode her red Schwinn bicycle on Massachusetts Avenue, rushing through traffic on her way to the Widener, or to Bickford's for tea and English muffins that dripped with salted butter, or back to the Radcliffe Quadrangle. Sun and seawater have discolored it, or perhaps this is how such hair ages. She wears a blue trapeze dress, buttoned down the front. It's sleeveless, and she has thrown over her shoulders a cable-knit cotton sweater of darker blue. Mistler dares to look at her legs. They are still fine, the ankles delicate. The high heels that announced her are the heels of fire-engine-red sandals. There is only one possible explanation. She is a guest. The real Bunny will appear in a moment.

Bella, he says, I am so glad. No, that's feeble. I am extravagantly happy! I had no idea. How could I have imagined you would be here, at lunch?

Barney, you useless dope! Didn't you explain to Thomas?

But I thought he knew. No, just the opposite. He told me he didn't know.

Bella, who are you?

Let's have some wine, she replies. Prosecco?

I can't possibly drink anything with bubbles, says Mistler. It has to be pure vodka or gin. Or red wine if that's easier.

She rings. The bell is next to the more vividly pink group of goddesses. Drinks are brought in.

Is it really true that I haven't seen you since college, Thomas? Just before I left for England?

Mistler nods. He has counted the years. Now he waits for an explanation.

I got married there, almost right away, to a man called Cutler. Thomas Cutler, in fact, but he was known as Tommy.

Like my father.

Bella smiles, and Mistler blushes at once. Circe turned men into swine; Bella turns him into an idiot. It has never failed. She smiles without letting her lips part, just as Mistler remembers it. The Mona Lisa smile. He guesses she hasn't done anything about those teeth, set too far apart.

Tommy was a very sweet boy, but a few years later he got the girl who really ran his gallery pregnant—he dealt in Islamic art—and wouldn't let her have an abortion. We hadn't managed to have a child, and he told me he was polyphiloprogenitive. I promise you! He is the only person I have ever heard use that word.

It's in T. S. Eliot, Barney informs her. One of the Sweeney poems.

That's where he must have found it. He always read with a dictionary at hand. For a moment, I was afraid it was some dreadful disease, and then I asked what it meant. His solution for the family problem was to throw me out. He was very firm about it. I left with my clothes. That's it! He needed everything else. Meanwhile, I had written some travel articles and a guidebook under the name Cutler, so I decided to keep that.

But why Bunny?

He couldn't stand Bella. When we met, he told me he wouldn't sleep with me unless I found another name. I was short on ideas, so I said call me You. He did, at first, but then he said it would be Bunny, because that's how I fucked! I must have told you that story, Barney, a thousand times. Anyway, Bunny stuck. Strictly *entre nous*, I think it rather suits me. It's easier to live up to than Bella! You see, Thomas, you will have to adapt! Will that be very hard, Thomas? You don't seem to have done any changing at all.

Learn the new name? I think I can manage in general conversation if you will forgive an occasional slip.

You always had everything very well under control in your head. That can't have changed either. Barney, you haven't told Thomas anything of my more recent history?

Oh, I think I did, last night, in my drunken stupor. What a pity he couldn't have seen you in full glory, in the family palazzo! That will be Joe, he added, at the sound of the terrible buzzer. I'll let him in.

Chatter in the vestibule. Mistler is filled with what is before him and what was in the past. He pushes aside a *Herald Tribune* to put his glass down on the coffee table and notices that it is made of a large discolored mirror. Bunny appears content to have him take her in so intensely; her smile is at that point where it might turn into a laugh. That's when she will gurgle like a turtledove. Instead, she winks at him. Thomas finds that very friendly. Here is Joe: he looks very young, but in this company that's easy. He must be past forty, though. A clean, candid face, very fresh white Brooks Brothers shirt, and blue jeans that must have just been washed, starched, and pressed. A nice fellow. He kisses Bunny on the cheeks three times and shakes Thomas's hand.

I am so glad to meet you, Mr. Mistler, you are such a legend.

Ouch, another creative part-timer from the bowels of an advertising agency. Their pay is too high. Why can't they sit in their cubicles or drafting rooms instead of being constantly underfoot. It's something worth mentioning at the next executive committee meeting. The thought of attending such a meeting is so absurd it visibly bucks Mistler up, and right away Joe thinks Mistler is likewise pleased to see him.

Really, he says, you've been such an inspiration!

Bunny comes to the rescue. Joe, you're so late, she says, that you don't deserve a drink. Let's sit down to lunch.

There is a lot of sauce on the pasta. Mistler likes how Bunny has tucked the corner of her napkin in where the dress closes tightly around her throat. Her throat is very full. Joe has a clever way of holding up his napkin with his left hand so that it covers that impeccable shirt front. It's a useful trick that Mistler at once imitates and plans to apply as well when eating green salad. Who says he can't change—if only he had learned how to do that in his youth, just think how many neckties would have been spared. Barney clearly doesn't give a shit. Gobs of brown drip on his black shirt. From time to time, he wets his napkin in his water glass and pokes at them. Mistler tells Bunny her wine is very good.

It's from the Feretti *azienda* in Friuli. Francisco-the-heir sends it over. He is very generous about wine.

It's the least he can do! cries out Barney. That boy should have let you keep the apartment and given you a pension!

He did offer me the one on the third floor, but it's dark. I like this better. Anyway, Enrico knew best who deserved what. Francisco did things for him he never got from me.

Joe titters. After a moment of reflection, Barney joins in.

How long are you staying, Thomas?

Only until Sunday.

What a pity! But you'll come back. Perhaps in the fall. That's when Venice is at her best.

She points across the canal to a bouquet of Tiepolo gray and pink clouds that make a half circle over the tower of San Trovaso.

I know. I've been coming here for years. I wish I had known that you were here. But I've never seen people. The idea was to look at things, read, and eat tiny young artichokes, like these.

Why did he not mention Clara? It will be even more awkward if he tries to repair the gaffe. Mistler can't bring himself to add, Oh and Clara is so passionate about Murano glass, though it would serve her right. He wishes he could skip buying the sherbet bowls. It's uncertain whether Barney has told Bella—that is, Bunny—about Mistler's condition; judging by her question, he hasn't. Delicacy of feeling and tact? He is perfectly capable of that. He could feel his way into an earth-

worm. Or worldly heartlessness? There is no reason to tell
your hostess, first thing in the morning, an unamusing piece of
bad news about a man you have invited to lunch without her
permission. Although something on the order of "I ran into
Mistler last night in that divine dive, yes, absolutely, the jock
with literary ambitions, he says he's dying from cancer, so I
asked him over" might have been all right too.

The artichokes are the accompaniment to broiled eel,
which followed the pasta. Very good food really, and a quartet
of hearty eaters: no wonder Bunny is no longer a svelte slip of
a girl. Still, both she and the boys seem in very good health.
They dig into a meringue pie that must have been bought at
the place next door. It's inconceivable that the motherly lady
with a wart on each cheek and the beginnings of a black goa-
tee, who waits on table and probably cooks as well, could have
made it. Might Bunny have a chef? From a habit he is determined to shake, Mistler takes only a half of the slice that's
presented to him. What's he trying to prove? That with a pull
here and a wince there he is still able to get into the clothes
he wore thirty years ago? Whereas you, my dears, just look at
you. To Mistler's surprise, the old lady passes the pie again.
He serves himself a huge chunk that, in the end, he can't
finish.

Joe doesn't work for Mistler's agency after all. He edits food
features for British *Vogue*. Why one would have an American
doing that when the Brits have taken over every job of that
sort in New York is worth investigating. Mistler puts the question. Ah, Joe is there to make sure the English taste is repre-
sented — for boiled mutton, bread sauce, meat pie, and public
school staples. English food writers are all into nouvelle cui-
sine! The great minds at the helm of *Vogue* think globally;

pigeonholing of talent is anathema. English food today, Picasso and German politics tomorrow. Joe seeks Mistler's advice on restaurants in Milan, his next port of call, and Paris, where there are bistros that still serve solid bourgeois food.

I leave that sort of thing for my hosts to worry about, is the churlish reply.

Then Barney chimes in to explain how a meal with Joe turns right away into a Chinese dinner, because he orders just about everything on the menu and wants to try what's on your plate, and from this and that it becomes clear that Joe is Barney's pal, not especially Bunny's.

The bearded lady has brought coffee, biscuits, and grappa. They move to the sofa and the armchairs facing it. Mistler finds he has been eating and drinking as though there were no tomorrow, which is, alas, the case. He studies Bunny's face, her eyes particularly, and hands, while Barney develops, presumably for Mistler's edification, an account of the last great party Enrico threw before he died. One has the sense that it's not the first time Bunny or Joe have heard it, and that he has regaled other audiences with it as well. The way Barney uses the pronoun "I" is the mirror image of how royalty says "we." It doesn't in the least mean he was alone. Indeed, unless the Greek goatherd had already alienated Leo's affection, Leo was surely with him at all the balls. Over the years, the story was that Barney had a conjugal existence. The way Joe nods his head knowingly and smiles in delectation, he too may have been in attendance, even if he is not included in Barney's first-person singular. Perhaps he has only listened to Barney tell the story before.

Baby, it was insane. The palazzo flaming with chandeliers on the canal side, torches in those gorgeous sconces at the gondola landing and at the entrance in the *rio*, banners the color of rubies with Feretti Venier arms hanging from every window! Maud Rodman asked me to take her to the ball. I said, All right, darling, but you simply must hire a gondola for the evening. Sublime weather! No wind! You could hear the oar slip in and out of the water. As soon as I arrived I saw how right I had been—everybody else came by water taxi. Quite a different effect. By the way, I am surprised Enrico didn't specify in the invitation "Guests shall arrive by gondola or on foot." Do you remember how in Rome, when he invited you to dinner, the invitation would read "Cocktails at nine, carriages at twelve"? That's my Enrico! I had an excruciating afternoon, going with Maud from shop to shop, while she looked for a mask to wear to the ball. Unbelievable! In the end, I told her, Baby, don't bother, your face is perfect as is, it's a death mask. Wear your black cape, and go as the Grim Reaper! She laughed and laughed. Just before the party, I went up to her suite at the Cipriani and helped her put on layers of rice powder until she looked like Marcel Marceau, only dead. I was wearing my Kabuki kimono, and when we walked from the landing up into the hall, everybody applauded. What a scene! Enrico's violin orchestra playing Vivaldi, waiters on every step of the great staircase holding trays of champagne and caviar on blini! Only Enrico would think of that. I began to look for you and Enrico. You were regal in green velvet and those insane Feretti pearls. When I asked about Enrico, you put your finger to your lips and looked mysterious. Remember? He made his entrance after midnight, with two mastiffs on a leash. Francisco told me later they had been watching television in his room.

They were his Irish wolfhounds. I begged him not to give the party. He was already much too weak.

But admit that it was pure Enrico to let the ball go on without him. Like the time in eighty-four, when he gave a lunch for Gianni in the garden on the Brenta. One hundred guests, tents, violins, divine decorations, a whole forest of magnolia flowers, and that black woman like the Queen of Sheba who sang Brahms. He never appeared at all! Finally, a message is received. From Capri! "I have gone to pay homage to our friendship on the island where Gianni and I first met, with the sea and the sun as my only colleagues." You read it after dessert was served.

Barney will never stop. There is no remedy; he is robbing Mistler of his last chance to speak to Bunny. He smiles at her and says he must leave. It's past his nap time. Just then, Fortune spins her wheel. Barney looks at his watch and says, Hey we're going with you. I made a date with the director of the Marciana library. He's giving us a private tour. Joe is coming. Why don't you and Bunny come too? It's in the Piazzetta, not far from your hotel.

Bunny to the rescue. Barney, why don't you and Joe run along. I know the Marciana very well. Enrico gave them a part of his collection. If Thomas can fight off sleep for a few minutes, I wish he would stay. It's been too long!

She rests her head against the back of the sofa and blows a series of concentric smoke rings. Ah, she hasn't lost the knack.

Ciao, ciao!

But not Mistler. Seated again, he gestures toward the bottle of grappa on the coffee table. A movement of the eyelids signals consent. He fills the glasses and takes out his cigar case. Another sign of acquiescence. Her eyes are very clear, darker blue than in his memory. Momentarily, he wonders whether she wears tinted lenses. Futile curiosity: the years of absence are like rooms with walled-up doors and windows. Not to be entered, even if he had worlds of time.

She moves to the end of the sofa, to be closer to him, puts out her cigarette, and says, Barney told me just before you came. It sounds very bad. Is it?

That sleepless whisper. Alps of cigarette butts. Let it be his requiem.

That's what I have been told. So far, most of the time I feel all right. Really, no different from before.

You're married, aren't you, and you have a child? Sometimes I read articles about you and all the important things you are doing. Of course, Barney has talked about working for you. You have been very generous. He makes it sound like a Guggenheim Fellowship for life.

Barney has a great gift, and I've been happy to see him use it. He is also an incredibly clever copywriter, worth every dollar we pay him. I do have a wife called Clara and a son called Sam. Sam is practically an old man, about to get married to a woman with a child that's not his. A little Hispanic girl.

Do you mind?

Lord no! I would have minded if he were alone.

And your wife? Why isn't she with you?

I came to Venice on an impulse, before telling her or Sam. To have a period of empty days. It turns out, though, that no such thing exists. Emptiness seems to turn into chaos, or the two are indistinguishable—at least in my case. Perhaps it's a general phenomenon.

Enrico worked until the very end. He refused to change anything in his routine. When I asked why he didn't stop, he said one only stopped if one thought one could use the time to be reconciled with God. Of course, he never worked for more than a few hours each day. That's not really true: the music was in his head all the time.

There is the difference. He was a great artist. My work is only another form of emptiness—structured emptiness!

Why do you say that? Haven't you built a huge business, given jobs to lots of Barneys and Leos? According to Barney, there is no one like you.

In my special business, there isn't, he is right about that. From another point of view, which happens to be mine, what I really do is use power, and those who do that are legion. I don't underestimate my skill, or the energy I used to have, or how well I have done what I set out to do. But power is like electricity. Very useful, if you want to turn the lights on. If you would rather let the room stay dark, it's nothing, simply a force that exists. In fact, when I go back to New York, I will make lots of lightbulbs burn for as long as I can, just to leave things in order. I will use power. But don't you see how very much one might want to stop using it? Whereas, if one had music or verses in one's head, one might want to hear them until there was no more sound. The idea I had for Venice was to let things happen, just once, without interfering.

That's rather how I have lived.

There you are. It's not purely a case of terminal sentimentality. So often, even when I was most concentrated on making things happen according to my plan, when I was at the peak of my form—in the use of power—a terrible longing would come over me for a different life. One used to think of the life I imagined as that of a beautiful woman: being attentive to herself and everyday things, available to some man, allowed, in fact encouraged, to be mildly irresponsible. Now that's an anachronism, so if I were to imagine again such a life it would be that of a beautiful, intelligent cat living in a house where everyone treats him well. Cats are the only gentlemen I know: they don't work for a living but are always occupied, they like games, they give their friendship as they please, and they don't take orders. They are elegant!

Thomas, you would have been an irresistible tomcat. Really, couldn't you have done anything you wished?

That's it. I wished and wished and saw to making my wishes come true. I became. Cats and beautiful women needn't do that. They are!

Then he could no longer contain himself. Bella, he told her, I wished for you. That's the wish that didn't come true. You broke my heart, you crushed me, you took away my hope. Why? Why did you love that man with the face of a camel? Why didn't you love me?

My darling Thomas, you amaze me! Do you mean Tim, poor Tim Lewis? I never loved him. He was someone I had fun with, that's all.

I mean the awful man with a long dreary face, greasy black hair, a premature bald spot, black-rimmed glasses, a fake trench coat, and black loafers so worn out they made you think his feet were wet.

She laughed. That was his talent agent look! He had a job with his uncle at MCA waiting for him after graduation. That's how he was going to get me a role in a movie, or at least a screen test, as soon as he started working. You wouldn't believe how badly I wanted to be in the movies! Much more than on the stage. I wonder what's become of Tim. He used to pass through London. The uncle had let him go and he took a job with the Voice of America. Or was it Radio Free Europe? I never knew which was which or what difference it made.

I don't care about Timothy Lewis's career. I don't care about his name. I care about the party in Lowell House after the Yale game. Stevie Merryman's party. The coats were in Stevie's bedroom. I was leaving and I went in to look for mine. The room was dark. I turned on the light. You were on the floor, on top of that fellow, screwing him. Your dress was hiked up all the way to your waist, so I could see how beautiful and white your back was. He had his trousers off, but not his jockey shorts or socks or those black loafers. I stood there for a minute since it didn't seem to bother you or him. Then I took my coat and left.

That wasn't very nice. I mean to stay to watch!

I was already good and crocked, but I poured myself another martini from the pitcher in the living room. Then I got my car and started for New York. Believe it or not, I wanted to see my father and ask him how such things could be, so he would tell me there was nothing hideously repellent about me. An idea that could have sprouted only in a drunk undergraduate's head. Still, that's what I was going to do. A few miles before Worcester, I went off the road, and the car rolled. Nothing serious, just a car that went to the scrap yard and a broken arm and shoulder. The cops found me. I was unconscious, but I guess they didn't smell the gin and they didn't make any trouble. That's what I remember.

I am so sorry, Thomas. In fact, I also remember that room and someone bursting in. I didn't see your face.

You were busy.

I was. I slept with a lot of boys when I was in college. What difference does that make? Why did it matter so much that you saw me? I never encouraged you.

No, you didn't. But why not? I used to wait for hours outside the Radcliffe library and then pretend I was just passing by when you came out. I would bring my bike, so I could ask if you would like to ride with me to Harvard Square, if you had your bike with you. If you didn't, I would leave mine, make believe I was on foot, and ask to walk with you. We would sit together on a bench in the Common and talk. Twice I asked you out to dinner, at the Henri IV, and you accepted. But I didn't dare to touch you or try to kiss you when I took you home. Once we held hands. That was all. I thought that was all you wanted. You made me think that. Yet you knew I was in love with you. Then why the camel's face and not I?

You frightened me, Thomas. You had all these things trailing behind you—your car, your racing bike, your fancy gabardine suits, your club tie, your trips to New York whenever the fancy struck you—but you weren't like the other rich boys who also rowed and were in clubs. One could make out with them and nothing happened. Sure, if you let them, they stuck a couple fingers inside you and came in their pants. Tomorrow would be another day. Or Tim. He'd screw you, make you come first, and then make you laugh about having a good time. With you there was nothing to laugh about. You were intense and timid, at the same time. I couldn't have expressed it then, but now I know: you were like a jealous husband without being married. Besides, everyone knew you were so goddamn bright. Don't make that face. If they didn't know, you made sure they found out. Thomas Mistler the perfect student and, let's face it, the big bore! I remember the time I showed you the poems I was writing. You asked to keep them overnight, and the next day you showed up at the dormitory and gave them back to me with your written comments and editorial changes. Like some section man! The awful thing was that your changes were good! You were right. That's what I couldn't stand. I wish I hadn't met you until we were both much older.

Your hair was ashes and gold. Your mysterious mouth. I know you were ashamed of your teeth. Your breasts. When I stumbled into that room, I wished you had been naked. I would have known your breasts.

Look now!

She unbuttoned the top of her dress and shook her shoulders free of it and the sweater. When she unhooked her brassiere, he saw that her breasts were huge and erect, like none he had ever seen.

Big, aren't they, she asked. Like ripe melons. If you like, you may touch them.

My hands are like ice, he answered.

You see? You haven't changed at all!

She began to touch her breasts herself, very delicately at first around the base. Once the nipples became erect, as though they would burst with blood, she interrupted the motion to squeeze them.

How the boys loved them, she crooned. I was the only girl at school with a bra that size. They would touch and lick them and I would come so hard, I've never come so hard again, never. You could have done that, Thomas, you could have played with them as much as you wanted, only you were so serious. I think I will come now, but it won't be the same, will it?

Bella, let me. Let me make you come. I want to touch them now. I really do.

Abruptly, she stopped.

It's too late. We aren't teenagers anymore. If we are going to make love it will have to be like two grown-ups in their late middle age.

Then let's. Please!

Not today. Barney will be back soon. Besides, you are tired. You see, she pointed at the bulge in his trousers, you wouldn't last one minute. Perhaps tomorrow. If you like, come to see me at lunchtime.

It wasn't quite six-thirty when he crossed the Accademia Bridge, continuing in the direction that would naturally lead him to the hotel. Just before the decisive turn, he looked at his watch and saw that he could, if he walked briskly, be at the Gesuiti before it closed. That is what he decided to do. Again the church was empty, and darker and sadder than during the visit with Lina. The grand, soaring interior struck him as uncomfortably small, like a house or public square one hasn't seen since childhood. In the reduced space, the white-and-gray-marble trompe l'oeil and, for that matter, the columns spiraling on both sides of the altar seemed intrusive, annoyingly artful. He shrugged his shoulders. His intention was, after all, only to have a last look at the great Titian. The conceits of eighteenth-century decoration had never been up his alley. He put a coin in the light box. Nothing. The painting remained in the shadow. Furious, he shook the box, then banged on it with his fist, and finally, defeated, fed the machine another five-hundred-lira piece he found in his pocket. That did it. Initial malfunction overcome, or proof of the good Fathers' business sense, for one thousand lire the halogen lamps went on. Yes, it was a very great work. Perhaps Titian's greatest, assuming such rankings made sense. For how could this painting be reasonably compared with the Venus at the Ca' d'Oro, or the Frari *Assumption* or the *Presentation of the Virgin* that he viewed with reverence each time he went to the Accademia? Had Titian invested less feeling in the little Mary standing forlorn but brave at the top of the stairs before the high priest than in Saint Lawrence on his grill? He was a master painter doing his job. Each of these different subjects required a different treatment as well as a different view on life, and it was not the smallest part of Titian's genius that he could provide it. All the same, he noted, as though he were verifying an inventory, how the torturer's fork was touching, but had not pierced, the saint's flank, the spiritual agony visible on the face of the assistant holding down the victim, and the brilliance of the spot of light on the mounted officer's helmet. Thereupon, the lamps went dead. Mistler had no more coins to feed them. Besides, his eyes had become accustomed to the dark. Whatever the reason, the painting did not seem noticeably more difficult to read. What he saw, however, did not move him. He might as well have been looking at an empty stage set.

[XI]

THE DAY HAD STARTED much too early. After breakfast, as soon as he was dressed, he went down to the lobby and made known to Signor Anselmo, the concierge, his wish to order flowers by telephone and have them delivered, before lunch, to a lady living on the Giudecca. The response lacked that official's customary enthusiasm and unction. For one thing, Mistler could not provide the lady's telephone number. Without it, how was the florist or Anselmo to make certain that Signora Cutler would be at home? Anselmo knew her; he also knew that she wasn't in the telephone directory.

She will be there, Mistler told him, and if she isn't, the man must wait.

By the time they finished going over the directions—Mistler's suggested route, which was to go over the Accademia Bridge to Dorsoduro, walk to the Zattere, and only then use the services of an ACTV vessel to cross the canal, having turned out, to his surprise, to violate Venetian notions of how one got from one place to another—and how the hotel *facchino* would carry Mistler's card to the florist and remain there, so that, in case no employee of the florist was available as soon as the bouquet had been made up, the very same *facchino* would bear the precious charge and wait in front of the door until the housekeeper or the *signora* materialized, Mistler had changed his mind. Since he couldn't fire the concierge the way he would have, without any waste of time, an equally obtuse and slow employee of Mistler, Berry, and certainly wouldn't deprive him of the tip he was used to receiving upon Mistler's departure, he would at least humiliate him.

I see that if I want Mrs. Cutler to have flowers at the hour I want her to have them, I must buy and carry them myself, he told Anselmo. That is what I will do. How strange that you can't manage such a simple task!

The reprisal had a calming effect on Mistler. Upon reflection, it came to him that he had never noticed flowers being delivered in Venice. Perhaps that wasn't the custom, except to church for funerals. No doubt, weddings as well. In reality, there was nothing wrong with taking care of this business himself. It might be pleasantly liberating to stop at the florist's shop on the way to Campo Santo Stefano. The flowers had caught his eye and so had the salesgirl. He was willing to bet she was an accomplished flirt. If only it were Sunday! That was when ladies and gentlemen of his age, and sometimes neatly dressed and combed young people as well, all of them one supposed on their way to lunch with in-laws or grandparents, could be seen walking, rather stiffly, bouquet in one hand and in the other a tart wrapped in a *pasticceria* paper. He might have felt he was part of the happy general population. Then it occurred to him that flowers, although she must definitely have them, weren't much of a memento of his visit, unless he were to buy one of those dried-flower arrangements he loathed. That way the flowers would serve also as a memento mori. Uncertain of what trifle of greater permanence to look for—scarves, belts, handbags, and the like all seemed inappropriate—he set off in the direction of San Marco. He lingered in front of the windows of stores that sold glass. Was it possible to give Venetian glass to someone who lived in Venice? In ordinary circumstances, he would have dismissed the idea as preposterous, but Barney had implied that all of Enrico Feretti's household possessions had gone to the boy. Certainly, he had not observed an abundance of sinuous handblown wineglasses or bowls on the lunch table. Under an arcade leading into the piazza, an almost impossibly elaborate pair of candelabra he had admired in the course of previous walks was on display in the window of an establishment that sold old glass as well as current production. Sea green and flecked with gold, their branches—he counted ten—were supports for tiny Moors, dressed in pantaloons, vests, and turbans, each presenting a different combination of colors, that hung on gold wires. In their tiny milk-white hands they held glass candles. The sherbet bowls Clara had asked him to replace came from this shop. Since he was already there, he decided he would buy them and the champagne glasses immediately, rather than in the afternoon, as he had planned. While his order was being written up, he asked the salesman whether it was possible to have a closer look at the candelabra. Visibly nervous about the task, the man covered a part of a counter with beige felt and cautiously put them on it.

Late eighteenth century, he told Mistler.

Really? In remarkably good condition.

Mistler found them even more astonishing than before. A month earlier, he might have wanted them for himself. As it was, why shouldn't this be his farewell present to Bunny? She had no cat to push them off the credenza or to bat with his paw at the baby Moors. They would give that disappointing living room a touch of real distinction—unless she decided to put them away in some dark corner precisely because she guessed what he had in mind and found that the grand gesture was, when you came right down to it, presumptuous, condescending, and out of place. Mistler thought the risk wasn't great, given the imminence of his eclipse. Who could possibly take offense at a romantic claim, however unwarranted, coming from him? If it turned out that he was wrong, and she was put out, it should be possible for a long-term resident of Venice like her to get this shop to take the candelabra back. His doubts resolved, Mistler told the salesman he was interested in a purchase. One moment, replied the clerk, I will have to ask the owner to see you.

An elderly gent appeared, more Levantine it seemed to Mistler than Venetian, and asked whether he could speak in French, in preference to English. Mistler nodded agreement.

These are very rare pieces, the man said, made by this house for the marriage of a member of the Albrizzi family just before Napoleon's army occupied Venice. The marriage took place, but in Padua, and the case containing the candelabra was found in the Albrizzi palace and unpacked only a few years ago. That's the reason for their remarkable condition. If it weren't for the difference in glassblowing technique and how one part of the candelabrum is joined to another, it would be easy to believe they were modern copies. If Monsieur would be kind enough to take the trouble to look.

He pointed with a finger that ended in a long, lacquered nail to details that Mistler agreed were interesting.

Really, they are fit for a museum, the Levantine continued. If possible, they should be offered to a bride.

Unfortunately, they won't be. And the price?

Less than you may fear. They are here on consignment. There has been much interest but no suitable collector willing to pay the amount originally asked.

He scribbled a sum in lire on a small piece of paper and next to it the dollar equivalent.

I don't know the market, murmured Mistler, but it's still a huge price. Much more cash than I can get for you today.

Monsieur may pay by check. Or we will send a bill. One has complete confidence in an amateur who understands the beauty of this work.

So be it. I want to take the candelabra with me. In fact, could you have them wrapped right now, perhaps individually, and have someone come with me, to carry them to the Giudecca, to the house of the lady to whom I will give them.

May I ask the name of the lady?

Mrs. Cutler. Possibly you know her. I hope you will allow Mrs. Cutler to return them in case they are not what she likes.

I guarantee to Monsieur that Signora Cutler-Feretti will never wish to part with them. Monsieur will forgive me for saying this, but, if it were in my power, they would indeed be her wedding present. Our house will be honored to reduce the price. I hope Monsieur does not find the gesture indiscreet.

An auspicious end to a morning of sorrow. Perhaps this attractive Alexandrian Jew—that was, it seemed to Mistler, his most probable identity—would be reunited with the candlesticks via the conquest of Bunny. So many worse things could happen to her.

In the nightmare from which he awoke so early, he had

been presiding over a meeting at a place that was familiar and yet not an office, at the head of an absurdly long marble-topped table, around which sat, while he addressed them, no, they were standing, men mostly known to him, whose names had faded from his memory. He was quite unable to make himself heard, although he raised his voice and spoke so loudly that his words echoed off the stone surface. He was quite powerless to affect the result, but it was essential to bring the session to a close: he was a prisoner there and expected urgently elsewhere, in a place he would not find without the restless, grimacing guide at the door shifting his weight from foot to foot. Ah, what anguish! It was past midnight in New York, too late to telephone Clara, however much he wished to get that daily task out of the way, and have nothing, literally no obligation, lying ahead. There was still time to call Sam in California, which he did. A party was in progress, judging by the background babble, unless it was some event on the television set, which had been turned up too loud or was too near the phone. Sam did not say he couldn't speak to him, but the awkwardness of the conversation increased as they talked. After each of Sam's replies Mistler felt the need to restart it, like cranking up an old car. Sam wasn't at fault. His responses were perfectly friendly. It was his patience that showed, like the hem of a slip one can't take one's eyes off. With that infinite patience, his son made the normality of his own situation clearly understood: work going well, both Monique's and his, no health problems affecting the household, the pleasant stretch of the weekend had just begun. That should have been enough, but it wasn't, and Mistler could not express what more he wanted. There was really nothing he could name.

The subject of pending obligations made him think of

Bunny's invitation, tacitly accepted when he left her. Had it been only a matter of having lunch with her for the second day in a row, the breach opened in his last day of freedom would have already been wide. In general, there is no need to have lunch or any other meal with the same person two days in a row, especially when it is an old friend who reappears, not seen in ages. After the initial outburst of curiosity and affection, what is there left? All that can be said has been said, and everything else is outside the boundary of verbal communication, can be apprehended in the best of cases only by witnesses living at one's side. A statute of limitations should bar attempts to renew intimacy once it has gone stale. But there was both more and less to Bella's invitation—he refused to succumb to the wit of the oaf who had renamed her and to think of her as Bunny. He had no doubt that he had understood her correctly: she meant to let him make love to her. Why? Because he had once wanted her with a force like despair? She was surely too wise to think that an afternoon's exertions could make up for what had been denied a lifetime ago, or to overlook the possibility that they might in execution prove disappointing. Since she was so intelligent, perhaps it was, in fact, her wish to show him the banality of the event, how it would be the same, by and large, with her as with any other woman, so that at the end of his life he would have nothing to regret on that score. The demonstration was useless. He had been in love with a girl in a tweed cape on a red bicycle who could not be brought back to the house on the Giudecca. If he followed Bella the Bunny to her bedroom, to sheets that she might have told the bearded lady to change for the occasion—more likely she hadn't bothered—he would find under his own knees and hands the knees and thighs of a remarkably well-preserved lady, but oh so different from the Walküre astride the man with the face of a camel. It could also be that she had suddenly found him attractive, the interest of his situation playing the pander. If that was it, had she noted the paradox? She was about to get a dying man to grant her a wish!

Years before, but at a time less distant than the afternoons they were accustomed to pass talking of literature and immortality in the comfort of the threadbare, overstuffed couch reserved for habitués of a Cambridge bookstore, Barney told Mistler about an obscure foreign writer of genius, whose novel he had read in a translation published by a press that was the usual outlet of last resort for such works.

He is writing this wild novel, said Barney, and all of a sudden the man realizes he doesn't know how to end it. What's he to do? Go on writing that mother for the rest of his life? So he runs to his old nanny, explains the situation, and asks her advice. She says: At the bottom of the page, right after the last word you have written, put down "Basta and pop! If you've read me you're a sop!" That will be your ending. Can you believe it? The weirdo does just that and goes on to write his next book!

Good counsel. Aren't novels said to be like a man's life? In that case there must be something other than "Hump the Bunny" to set down at the bottom of his last page. He might simply fail to present himself on the Fondamenta San Biagio and instead, in due course, send her a postcard from New York so conceived that she could, if she chose, conclude that Mistler had not caught on, that he thought she had dismissed him. Even better, he would send her flowers timed to arrive at midday with a note to the same effect. The advantage lay in sparing her the annoyance of a long wait in her bower for a no-show swain. In case she called the hotel to set him straight, she would learn that Mr. Mistler had gone to Torcello and was not expected until the late afternoon.

By eight o'clock, the hour at which he felt he could no longer bear to keep postponing his breakfast, his resolve to pirouette and depart had become firm. It was only a matter of waiting until shops opened so that he could order the roses. He thought that nineteen of the reddest and longest, a dozen and a half plus one to make an odd number, would be just right. The waiter had brought in the newspapers deposited earlier outside his door. The news in the *Herald Tribune* would be no staler if left until the evening, nothing bored him more than the campaign of two presidential candidates for whom he had equal loathing, except, possibly, business news. He did, however, sneak a look at the closing price of Omnium. Up two dollars! That could add spice to the talk he was to have with Jock Burns. He picked up *Il Gazzettino*, saw that the weather forecast was as satisfactory as the blue sky outside his window, and turned to the horoscope. At the sign of Taurus, which was his, he read: "You will be tempted to turn your back on a friend. Expect to be judged according to your actions. Your health is unchanged."

Ah, the superb decrees of Minos! Soon he would have more to tell about them than this astute astrologer had ever learned from the stars, if only dead men could talk. For the moment, the admonition was too stern to be ignored. He would play his cards as they lay.

That is how Mistler found himself on the accustomed route that led, ambiguously, to the restaurant where the waiters, assembled like cherubim, would set before him a meal, for the quality of which he would have put his hand in the fire, that he could consume, his face lifted toward the rays of the sun, in undisturbed tranquillity, or to a destination a mere hundred meters farther and a consummation of a different order. The Alexandrian Jew's employee followed, a big square box in each hand. Mistler carried the roses, heads down, as he had been taught was best. Together they boarded the vaporetto, together they disembarked, shrugging their shoulders in unison, not at Sant' Eufemia, as they had expected, but at the Giudecca, one bridge away, where the vessel had whimsically stopped.

Un tormento, averred the employee.

You're telling me, kid.

They walked and walked. Heels, knees, and legs, and more heels, knees, and legs, walking and walking up to the crown of the bridge and down from the crown of the bridge, and again. The point of no return was reached — the little church of Sant' Eufemia. Disaffected or merely abandoned, its locked doors bearing no mention of hours of worship, plastered with layers of posters. This was the moment for Mistler to ask the *facchino* to set down his boxes, rest a visiting card on top of one of them, draw a line across his name, and scribble underneath it "Ciao Bella." Let the boy carry it all to the *signora,* the boxes, the roses, and the card. If he pulled a long face about the flowers, Mistler would relieve him of the bouquet and hand it to the first old lady he came across on his way back to the vaporetto. Oh, Bella! Would she order the messenger to take his wares back where they came from or, worse yet, to Mr. Mistler himself? He had no doubt she knew how to make one feel her scorn. "My dear Thomas," she would write, perhaps on the back of his own card. "How sad! Have you done this out of fear, cruelty, or plain bad manners?" Unless, of course, she had foreseen it all and was not at home, her door barricaded or guarded by the lady with a beard.

He felt very hot; in fact, his head was spinning. Under the double-breasted blazer, as of this morning too heavy, altogether wrong for the season, his shirt stuck to his back. He unbuttoned the blazer, handed the flowers to the boy, and taking hold of the lapels fanned himself. Ugly wet spots covered his shirt front. A glowering large man in dark clothes perspiring uncontrollably, his face bloodless and tinged with ugly yellow. That's how he was, that's how he would present himself to her. He had noted the hue while shaving and confirmed it, taking off his sunglasses, studying the reflection in the store windows he had passed on the way. To return to his room, close the shutters, and lie down on the bed in the airy half darkness. He would not move until nightfall, or, better yet, if he swallowed a couple of Bill Hurley's pills, if they struck his nerves once more with their hammer blow, not until the next morning. Then indifferent, blinking against the sunlight, he would pack his bags, descend to the cashier's desk, wait while the computer ground out the monstrous bill, and begin his voyage homeward.

He gave up wiping his face with the silk square taken from his breast pocket. Diarrhea in a Turkish toilet. Like a shadow, the employee stopped wiping his on his sleeve. It's very warm, he commented.

I should have taken a water taxi, but as it is we had better keep going.

They are so expensive! Really a robbery! It's best to take the vaporetto at San Zaccaria.

The uniformity of the natives' views was impressive. Too bad! His own search in Venice had been for the pleasures of the eye. Efficiency had counted for very little. In the end, though, it was all the same; his feelings and perhaps even memories were coming to a dying fall, like a sustained, heartrending violin note one hears through some open window just before the unseen hand, for reasons one will never know, puts down the bow.

They had climbed to the top of the little bridge. At the bottom of the steps on the other side stood Bella, candid and smiling.

The buzzer is broken, she informed him. First I waited outside my building, but it's boring there. I was on my way to the vaporetto stop and street life. What beautiful roses! I think they are for me.

She tilted her head and offered her cheek.

Forgive me. You don't want to be kissed by a sweaty tourist.

Then hurry to the house. Angelina closed the shutters just in time. It's divinely cool.

She noticed how he took in her dress, a long shapeless garment almost transparent from the waist down, of the sort he associated with Laura Ashley and civil rights marches. It revealed an undergarment rather like the bottom of an old-fashioned two-piece bathing suit. On her feet, Scandinavian wood clogs, with red leather uppers.

Aren't you amused? Not the least bit? I thought I would make you think of the sixties! Almost our era. Besides, she whispered, looking out of the corner of her eye at the shop employee, it unbuttons all the way!

You are marvelous! Who else would have thought of it? I should have worn chinos and dirty white bucks!

But Mistler wasn't amused. Overt lasciviousness revolted him, like seeing a waiter, at a second-rate buffet, pile on a guest's plate, already heaped with fish in cream sauce, servings of green salad and runny Brie. But that was not the only reason. In 1970, in August, while Clára and Sam were at Crow Hill, he had gone to dinner with Peter and Jill Berry and Jill's cousin, recently divorced, at an Italian restaurant on Lexington Avenue, across from Bloomingdale's, which was then thought both raffish and chic, just the place on a hot summer night for a fashionable young couple, an unaccompanied young woman, and their summer-bachelor best friend, invited to balance the table, to find themselves. The place was always noisy, insufferably crowded, reservations had no value, and the trick was to catch the eye of the owner, slim and imperturbable in a suit that was made for him in Rome and made the diners' clothes look like cheap stuff bought off the rack. Their presence was acknowledged by the great man with a good-humored nod, which, according to convention, meant that they would get their table fairly soon, but only after a probationary passage at the bar. They drank martinis from glasses so full the liquor spilled on their fingers. The cousin had long hair, round eyes, and droopy breasts. Mistler had not yet caught her name and wondered whether Peter was sleeping with her. To make herself heard over the roar of voices, she spoke about her work right into Mistler's ear. He liked her breath, which smelled of cigarettes and gin, her strong white teeth, and how she knew to stand not more than an inch away from him without letting their bodies touch. She wore no lipstick. Later, over grappa, Peter said Peggy's former husband was a low swine. It was a relief that she had finally got rid of him. He proposed a toast to her freedom.

Peter and Jill walked home, leaving it to Mistler to take Peggy back to Chelsea, at the other end of town. In the taxi he discovered that her mouth was as enterprising as pleasant. Without a word, he followed her upstairs to the apartment on the top floor of a redbrick town house.

Take your shoes off, she said at the door. I want to make sure Jeb is all right.

That was a surprise. Mistler raised his eyebrows.

That's right, you don't know. He's my son and partner. A great little guy.

There was nothing the matter with Jeb. Her bedroom, most of it occupied by what looked like an oversize waterbed covered by a quilt, was down the corridor from his.

I hate making my bed, she told Mistler. This is my lair.

What if Jeb wakes up?

He won't. Or he will and I will tell him you are a very special friend.

When he was leaving, she said, Peter is your sidekick. I don't want him to know.

I don't either. We can have fun, if this is only between you and me.

He saw her during the rest of the summer sporadically, when she summoned him. She explained variously that she couldn't afford a baby-sitter and didn't like to leave Jeb alone, or that there was no baby-sitter whose presence in the apartment she or Jeb could bear. She preferred not to go out; the evening with the Berrys had been an exception. Wait until Jeb has a weekend with his father, she told Mistler. In the meantime, they dined with Jeb, who was Sam's age, but unlike Sam went to sleep early and without having to be coaxed. Then she did the dishes and led Mistler to the bed. It was Mistler's first experience of a woman who didn't consider it a condition to having sex that he telephone her and propose this or that entertainment.

If you feel like fucking, she told him, you can call and ask to come over and I will tell you whether I'm in the mood. If I were you, I wouldn't bother. When I want it, I'll be in touch.

That was all right with Mistler. In fact, he liked not having to ask himself whether he should have called her when he hadn't. She would get hold of him at the office, his secretary, the exquisitely sensitive and discreet Miss Tuck, having no doubt that Peggy's calls should be put through or, if Mistler was not alone, promptly returned.

During the last weekend of August, Mistler was in Crow Hill. The telephone rang in the early evening on Saturday. Mistler picked up the receiver in the living room, where Clara and he were having a drink. It was Peggy, and yet he had not given her his number in the country. He did not think that telephoning him there was a part of their compact.

Hey, come into the city early on Sunday. Jeb is with his father on the Cape. I want you to take me to the movies and then to dinner.

I'm tied up now, replied Mistler, noting that Peggy's voice had remarkable carrying power, I'll get back to you later.

No, you're not! If you were tied up, you couldn't have answered the phone. Giggle giggle. You had better come, I want you real bad.

Clara had not looked up from her magazine. Was she utterly absorbed by fall fashions? Mistler thought it was more likely the hair-spray effect of her good breeding.

When he called back a little later from his study, Peggy told him to meet her at the theater, off lower Fifth Avenue. He went there straight from the train, arriving a little early, bought the tickets, and waited outside the lobby. It was a Warhol film. It seemed to Mistler that the fans in the queue of

ticket holders were about what one would have expected—
Upper West Side bookkeepers, doctors from the boroughs with
artsy wives, a punk or two hired by the distributor as a come-
on. At last she appeared. He had never seen her in anything
but blue jeans and men's shirts, and the little linen sleeveless
dress she had worn the evening with the Berrys. This time she
was sauntering toward him, her face no less candid than
Bella's, wearing a dress that was a dead ringer for Bella's, and
clogs. One point of difference: Peggy's clogs were brown. They
drew attention to her feet, fleshy and calloused and not totally
clean, which was not surprising, since she had probably
walked all the way from Twenty-third Street.

They necked during the movie, her legs, which she had liberated from the dress, wrapped as far as possible around his.
Afterward she said she wanted to eat on the terrace of a hotel
restaurant a few blocks away. That was good news for Mistler;
the chances of anyone he knew having dinner there were
remote. Fifth Avenue was almost empty. Perhaps for that reason, she hung on his arm and leaned against him while they
walked. To his shame and horror, Mistler realized that if
someone he knew did see them, he would feel more seriously
compromised by her slatternly appearance than by the show of
intimacy. The evening ended energetically, according to the
established formula, except that, instead of fleeing in the middle of the night to avoid being found by the great little guy in
his mom's bed and having to listen to the explanation of his
presence, Mistler remained in bed until breakfast, climbed
once again on top of Peggy, shaved with the razor she used on
her legs (but not armpits, which, unexpectedly for a girl of her
background, she left hairy and moist), and went directly to the
office. Without a word having been said, Miss Tuck altered

her way of dealing with Peggy's telephone calls. It didn't matter. Soon afterward, Peter told Mistler that she had married a physics professor and moved to L.A.

And these elegant boxes are for me as well? asked Bella. They can't possibly hold gloves or books. Thomas, you haven't had this young man bring your luggage? No? Then it must be a week's provisions from Harry's Bar!

No, Bellissima, not this time. If you like, this gentleman will carry the boxes upstairs and unpack them too.

Then I will keep my eyes closed until he has finished.

When the candelabra had finally been placed on the credenza, as he intended, and he had told her she had better take a look, it seemed to Mistler that she blushed.

Thomas, she said, I know them. Monsieur Benamoun has told me over and over they would be sold only to a client who deserved great happiness.

He has kept his word. I let him know they were for you.

He saw that the table at the window, where lunch had been served the day before, was not set. On the coffee table, though, there were bottles and glasses.

May I have a drink? he asked. Something rather strengthening and full of vitamins, like gin? I found the walk here hot, and unusually tiring.

Wouldn't white wine with soda be better? We don't want you to feel sleepy, do we?

Don't we? Why was she goading him? Let not the gift of old glass become the prelude to the enactment of a grotesque Mask. A queenly figure of great beauty, in scant and diaphanous attire, appears surrounded by summer's riches. The mouth of a dying man is pressed to her bounteous breast. Parched with thirst, it receives the white arc of milk her mild hand presses from it. Gratitude or Charity? Vanish, Lina, get thee behind me. If he had made Bella happy, it would be the first action since he arrived in this watery graveyard that he needn't regret. Her way may be simply how nice people with good hearts go about making love. What right had he to spoil the show by a fit of temper? Therefore, he poured the gin, stirred it with ice, drained the glass, and told her, Ah, my beautiful Bella, don't worry. Nothing can take my mind off you.

Her hand on the inside of his thigh, the gesture repeated: she opened her dress and shook her shoulders free of it. She was bare.

Here, they are yours.

Because he had turned toward her and was quite immobile, she added, Don't make me wait. I can't bear to wait.

Afterward she smiled at him brightly and said, What a loving man! I will be right back.

I think I need more of your gin.

She returned with an ice-cold towel.

Wipe your face with it first. You are so red.

I know. Swollen face and hands, bloodshot eyes. Your trophies. Please, stay just like that, leave your dress open. I don't want to stop seeing you.

You're silly, Thomas. Wait for me in that chair. Already you look more comfortable.

Follow her into the bedroom. They would undress. Probably, she would want to undress him; she had nothing on except that dress and the modest panties it revealed. There was nothing wrong with his body. He was glad at the thought of being seen. And hers? There would be the mound of her stomach, probably milky and unlined, the advantage of not having borne children. He did not think he would dislike it. And all the rest to be touched, probed, and licked. This time she would want him inside her; she would try to help. Waiting for it to happen. Those gestures that would revive him the soonest were exactly the ones he must avoid. In the end, she would be lovely about it, tell him that to hold each other is enough. In a while, he would hear her in her bathtub. Would you like a nice cool bath too? With me, or are you too big? If only this were the Savoy, with those huge tubs. You were made for them or they were made for you! Bella, he had better say, I am not the man I was. I feel my age even more than it shows. And then?

When she came back to the living room she had on white cotton trousers and a dark tunic.

You're dressed up!

Of course. We are going out to lunch.

But Bella!

No more today. Don't pretend you want to. Thomas, I am glad to have those candelabra. I will think of you each time I look at them. They will stay right here, under that portrait of a man with an earring, which may be really a Longhi. She giggled. Now I am going to give you a keepsake, but it's one you will have to hide.

He saw that she had a pair of small scissors in her right hand. With the other one she grasped a strand of her hair, cut it off at the roots, and made a knot.

Bella, he moaned.

I wish it weren't gray. Now come along. I am starved.

By the time they took their coffee the terrace was empty. The white umbrellas made a clapping noise in the breeze like sails needing to be trimmed. What is she like, she asked, your wife.

Clara? I am not sure I can tell you. It's as though she won't stay in focus. That happened to me once with Japanese binoculars I bought to look at birds at the feeder through the window of my study. They weren't quite good enough; I've never gotten satisfaction from small economies. One moment, I saw every detail, the corner of the finch's eye, tiny imperfections in his beak when he opened it to take a grain, and then, all of a sudden, he would become a blur. Clara? She was beautiful and suitable, and everything about her went with the way I thought things should look. A tall blond girl of good family with no money, making her own way in Manhattan. Two good dresses and unfailing good humor. Thereupon, I appear, I am somewhat glamorous, and, of course, such a catch. She knows it, but doesn't let it matter too much because she has that sort of pride. We make love and she tells me, when it's over, she has never gone all the way before, but there is no fuss about what happened, she doesn't ask for any pledges. That really hooked me!

Did you love her?

You might as well ask whether she bored me from the start. Did I, in my patronizing way, think that being bored in a marriage was normal? Love? I think I have loved only one woman, a woman I never had and never lost. That was my father's mistress. I might have loved you, if you had let me. But you didn't. What matters about Clara is that probably I spoiled her life. She should have waited for the next heavy beau.

How did you spoil it?

She came to see I didn't respect her. Never mind that she put herself in the wrong. By the way, I didn't respect my mother. My son doesn't respect Clara.

You have brought him up badly.

By setting a bad example? Surely. But she didn't do well with him either.

Does your son love you?

I think so, but he doesn't find it easy.

Then I think you and Clara have spoiled each other's lives. Pointlessly. Do you want to come back to my place? No, don't answer, it would be a mistake to do it now. Come back instead at the end of the summer.

By then, I will be dead, or very sick.

Come back, even if you are very sick.

He took the vaporetto to the other side, his eyes fixed on Bella until she became a very small figure. Once on the Zattere, he headed toward the Dogana, the prow of Venice, where salt, one of the riches of the state, had once been stored. At metal tables in front of the two cafés, tourists ate pizza, tired sandwiches of ham and tomatoes, and ice cream. Others sat on the pavement, leaning against the garden walls. Young Nordic men with bare chests turning scarlet, the litter of their running shoes and socks scattered about them, girls exposing their thighs and shoulders to the sun. Ugly flesh, smell of rancid oil, water thick as sewage, his own body terribly heavy. Walk, walk, and walk. Impossible to sit down beside them. He would not rest until he had rounded the Dogana and reached Santa Maria della Salute. Then, if the basilica was open, he would pause on a bench before the Black Madonna, take one more look at the headless, bloody trunk of Goliath in the Titian ceiling. He couldn't remember whether the men who worked the oars of the *traghetto* gave up their labors after lunch or returned for an hour or two at the end of the afternoon. Terrible loneliness and fatigue. Mighty Hermes, guide of travelers, send them to their task! Don't make your servant climb once more the iron-edged steps of the Accademia Bridge, spare him the passage through the crowd of timid Senegalese, each as beautiful as a Veronese come alive, chattering among their wares in the arid vastness of Campo San Stefano. Walk, walk, walk. He reached the boathouse of the Bucintore rowing club, a building away from the Dogana. Like the sound of vesper bells that mourn the dying of the day and pierce a pilgrim's heart with desire, the smell of varnish and fresh wood filled him with great longing. The huge doors of the boathouse were open. He stopped to admire the sleek single sculls and racing eights sleeping on their racks, mythic beasts he had loved so much. On a chair, repairing an oarlock, sat a small, dark-skinned man wearing navy-blue sweatpants and a red T-shirt with the insignia of the club. Another Moor, thought Mistler. The man considered him carefully. A moment passed.

You like these boats, he observed.

Molto.

Ah, you are English? An oarsman, I am sure.

The accent was redolent of India. Mistler took in the man's fine, small features. He was old, older than Mistler, fit and very strong.

No, I'm American. I used to row.

It shows. There is no used to row for a man of your build and your hands! He laughed. You look and sound like an Englishman. If you like, come here tomorrow. The boats go out on Sunday morning. We will see. There may be a place for you. If a member has been inconvenienced, the crew will be honored to welcome such a guest.

Thank you. I am leaving Venice tomorrow.

Then the next time.

Yes, certainly.

He waved goodbye. Immobile, the man smiled.

Minutes later, already at the Dogana, Mistler stopped to look carefully at the passage between San Giorgio and the Giudecca. He retraced his steps. The next time. What if this were a sign? The Eastern man was back in his chair, working on the oarlock.

Tell me, asked Mistler, these single sculls. Are there any that can be bought? I haven't rowed with a crew since I was a very young man. I prefer being alone on the water. When I return, I might like to take out a scull from time to time.

There are no sculls for sale. You would have to get to know a member well enough to have him lend his scull to you.

What a pity.

As Mistler began to walk away, the man cried out: Sir, why speak only of sculls? Would you be interested in a wherry? Please come with me.

Mistler followed. Squat, and shiny black like a long coffin, the boat lay in the back room.

It's like one I had when I was a boy, he told the man. I used it out on the bay, in the place where I still live. It was very steady. Only mine wasn't painted black. It was varnished, like your sculls.

This one is very steady too, sir. The owner wanted it painted black, like a gondola. He passed away last year. Now it is mine.

Yes, Mistler recognized the virtues of the wherry. One might go to sea in it when the days grew short, in the early evening, an hour or so before sunset, just as the wind fell. The end of the Giudecca to starboard, pass out of sight and out of mind. Ahead lies the Lido. At its end, San Pietro in Volta, the attendant island. Between them the narrow passage of

Malamocco. Slow strokes of inexorable strength. Head into the wake of barges at a slant. The wind freshens, in half an hour the smell of the open sea. The last rays of the sun in your eyes, the prow points at the place from which the moon will rise. The watery space is vast.

You use her much?

Oh no sir. I have been thinking I might sell.

Then sell it to me please. And will you keep it here until I return?

With pleasure.

Two important purchases in a day. Mistler put his hand in the inside pocket of his blazer where he kept his checks.

No need to do that, sir. You may pay me when you return.

I may be delayed. Let me pay now.

Then step into my office. This chair. Make yourself comfortable.

The boatman sat down on the other side of the desk in the room that was black like the wherry; his eyes burned. He watched Mistler write. Then, writing slowly himself, he recorded the transaction in a large book. His face pleasant but grave, he handed Mistler a receipt. Everything was in perfect order. Mistler's obol had changed hands. This time he would not cheat.

Mistler's Exit

Louis Begley

A Reader's Guide

A Conversation with Louis Begley

Q: The notion of leaving America and losing oneself in a foreign country is an intriguing element in your work. Can you explain it?

LB: Although the notion that my books are autobiographical has the persistency of a young dog trying to climb onto the sofa, none of them is a disguised memoir. They are simply, like all serious works of fiction, made out of the author's experiences, thoughts, and feelings. I came to the United States when I was thirteen, as a refugee from Poland, a "displaced person." No matter how hard I have tried to become American and how successful in this effort I may have been, I am still a "displaced person" in the largest sense. Perhaps all writers are, but in my case the displacement has retained its geographical aspect. It is also the case that I have traveled frequently and widely and that my experiences outside of the United States have been intense, not those of a tourist. Leaving and disappearing are natural to me, like disguises. It doesn't surprise me, therefore, that my principal characters also find it natural to move around: Ben in *The Man Who Was Late* quite literally escapes to France from a broken marriage. Afterward, he feels that the sidewalks of New York burn his feet. He escapes from Paris to Rio de Janeiro because he cannot face the implications of deep involvement with a woman who loves him desperately, whose love he in fact returns. Max, the narrator of *As Max Saw It*, is merely peripatetic. There is no particular significance in his meeting Toby and the great Charlie Swan in a villa on the Lake of Como or in his reconnecting with them in the Forbidden City in Beijing. Schmidtie of *About Schmidt* is, in fact, a homebody. He shuttles between Bridgehampton, in Long Island, and Manhattan. And Mistler! Poor Mistler knows there is no escape from the crab devouring his liver but he wants a moment of grace and irresponsibility before he must face his wife and son for the last time, before he crosses the river Styx. Like Ben, he flees, but for different reasons. He chooses Venice, the most beautiful city in the world, a watery, pink and gray Gothic graveyard. Can you blame him?

Q: Mistler is engineering a wildly lucrative sale of his advertising company, and his will to close the deal seems undiminished when he discovers that he has terminal cancer. Has your career in law and high-level business transactions given you special insight into the psychology of people at the top?

LB: I hope so! Otherwise I have been wasting my time. Discipline, the ability to carry on and get what you want no matter how awful you feel, are the means and the price of ascent. Terrible personal adversity often serves as a stimulant. You may have also noticed something I happened to be interested in showing: how one conducts two activities at the same time. For instance, Mistler's idle chatter with the young photographer Lina Verano, who pursues Mistler all the way to Venice for sex and a chance to photograph him, goes on while he figures out the impact of the deal he's making on his estate tax.

Q: Mistler describes his immensely successful career as "structured emptiness." Is the hollowness he feels entirely attributable to his own nature—could he have ever been happy? Or might one also infer something about the nature—and price" of success in our culture? Are we all vulnerable to such feelings?

LB: I take issue with your assumption that Mistler is fundamentally unhappy. In fact, at the beginning of the book, the reader is told that he "considered himself a happy man, as the world goes." That is, of course, before he has spent a week or more acquainting himself with the cancer colonizing his liver, before he has gone to Venice and looked into the abyss. And when he tells Bella, after a boozy lunch, that his "work is only another form of emptiness—structured emptiness!" I am inclined to think the reader should listen with a mixture of respect and skepticism. Note the forces that are at work. First of all, Mistler talks well, and likes to listen to himself. How much of what he has just said is phrase making? Second, he has a well-bred WASP's normal penchant for self-deprecation. In this instance it would seem to have been put into overdrive by what Bella has just told him about the way

Enrico, her late husband, faced death. Enrico was a great artist; Mistler's writing career never got off the ground. Mistler surely dislikes the thought that he will be measured against the husband. A natural defense would be to make the comparison *a priori* untenable. Third, isn't Mistler caught in an extraordinary emotional turmoil, the memories of his hopeless infatuation with Bella literally crowding out the room?

The doubts I have tried to sow do not invalidate the basic question about a career such as Mistler's. I would say that my protagonist is afflicted by an excess of lucidity, which leads him to see his huge success in business as nothing more than the equivalent of winning at a superbly complicated game. A game, moreover, that is worth playing only at immense speed and if a maximum of risks is taken. This is a way that some brilliant, lucky players—fundamentally indifferent to material rewards of success but devoted to other values and vistas—judge their accomplishments. I do not think that all businessmen are vulnerable to such feelings or that a judgment about our culture should be inferred. Rather, I believe that Mistler presents a special case, epitomizing men and women who are obsessed by the vanity of all human endeavor that does not have some transcendent purpose. One such purpose in Mistler's understanding, would be the creation of a great work of art. A different man in Mistler's position would look back on his life and accomplishments and quite honorably congratulate himself.

Q: **Like *Death in Venice*, *Mistler's Exit* is both a love letter and a meditation on mortality. What inspiration, if any did you draw from Thomas Mann?**

LB: The question is impossible to answer. Thomas Mann, like Proust and Henry James, like the ghosts of so many others, is always there. They crowd the corners of the room. Mistler of course knows with a certainty that he is going to be dead very soon. In this he differs from Aschenbach. He goes to Venice to taste the forbidden fruit of irresponsiblity, freedom and emptiness, and, he hopes, pleasure of the senses (looking at paintings and buildings he loves, not sex!), before he must enter the war zone of dying. Poor Aschenbach thinks Venice will restore him.

Q: **Mistler's marital and professional choices have always been conventional, yet his decision to flee to Venice when he learns he is dying is out of character for him. What makes Mistler tick?**

LB: You have to read the novel—carefully—to find out! The bare bones answer may be in the comment he makes to Barney Fine in the barroom scene: his genetic puritanism. Combined with a curious mixture of an overpowering need to be the first, especially among equals, and his existentialism. Mistler believes that a man's life is his sum total, his complete definition.

Q: *About Schmidt* **seemed to sound the death knell of the American Establishment, but in** *Mistler's Exit,* **the WASP plutocracy seems still ascendant, or at least alive and kicking. Is there still an Establishment that works in the manner Uncle Abthorp describes, or have the past couple of decades forever altered the traditional paradigm of money and power?**

LB: Don't forget that Uncle Abthorp delivers his lecture on Old and New Money a long time ago, say in the late 1960s, when Mistler, Lovett & Berry have hit their stride. Schmidtie, on the other hand, takes stock of New York society in the 1990s. Much had changed during those momentous intervening decades. Nevertheless, Uncle Abthorp's views remain valid.

Take the cultural institutions he recommends to his favorite nephew as hunting grounds of choice. If you peruse their annual reports, you will see boards of directors that are bouquets delicately composed of different types: colossally rich new men and women, the ones who, according to Uncle Abthorp, have kept their money and are able to "fit in"; the not nearly as rich old Establishment types, whose presence makes the new boys and girls feel they have really and truly made it in society; and the "trophy" members. Into this last category fall intellectuals or artists or persons who pass for such, whose role is to amuse and educate the others—think of the role of Athenian slaves in imperial Rome—to make them feel that charity can be fun. And, indeed, the new rich have gotten their seats by giving and giving and giving.

Effective power has slipped from the hands of the WASP plutocracy (except of course for those few members of the old elite who have remained very rich), but not the power to anoint, to give the new rich a certain gloss and increased respectability. That is why Mr. and Mrs. New Money collect the old rich, even as they constitute great art collections, acquire historic dwellings, and take up polo and the most expensive of blood sports. The pattern is not novel. After all, so many of the grandest old WASPs descend from robber barons of the end of the last century and their hangers on. Those worthies knew that in a democracy, since you can't become a prince or a marquis, you had better found a museum, give to charities, and shine as a patron of the arts.

Q: **One is continually startled by the elemental sexuality that invades the decorous atmosphere of your novels. What is the significance of this counterpoint?**

LB: There is a considerable amount of powerful sex in my novels because I think the sexual drive exerts an overpowering influence on us. Beyond procuring pleasure, it opens us to one another, it ripens us much as the sun ripens green fruit. Indeed I have always thought that sex is the only proven means of breaking out of our solitude. That is more important than sex as a means of exerting power.

Q: **One of the most moving elements of the novel is Mistler's relationship with his son, Sam. What have you learned about fatherhood through writing this novel?**

LB: How one never does anything right, how almost every well-intentioned action miscarries, how nothing can be truly repaired. Parental love is tragic; the relationship necessarily ends in loss. One's adult children are fatally different from the childhood images fixed in one's memory; they may be splendid, but they are different, and in the meantime one has become an old man. If one is lucky, one will receive from the son the rite of forgiveness, as Mistler hopes he will receive it from Sam, perhaps because he has accepted so totally what time has made of that once beautiful child who is his only son. I always have in mind those lines in Yeats's "Among School Children," where the poet asks himself what woman would think the shape of her son with sixty of more winters on its head a compensation for the pain of his birth or the uncertainty of what awaits him.

When it comes to their emotions, fathers and mothers aren't all that different.

Q: **Where do you see *Mistler's Exit* in the development of your novels since *Wartime Lies*? What's next for you?**

LB: I hope I have made progress in learning the novelist's craft. My themes have remained the same: our dreadful isolation (Proust put it unforgettably when the narrator learns his grandmother is dying: *Chaque personne est bien seule*), and how only love and solidarity can help us break out of our isolation; men's indifference to other men, which is the bland mask of cruelty; death as our absolute ending.

Before I reach that ending, I would like to write more novels. The one I am beginning to write is actually a temporary resurrection. I intend to bring back Schmidtie, the crotchety protagonist of *About Schmidt*, and his magnificent friend, Carrie.

Questions and Topics for Discussion

1. Mistler considers himself "a happy man, as the world goes," yet when he receives his fatal diagnosis, we are told "preposterously, unmistakably he began to rejoice . . . [feeling] he had been set free." How are we to account for this strange reaction? How does it take on meaning as the novel develops?

2. Once he learns about his illness, Mistler tries to change the terms of his firm's merger deal without informing Jock Burns of the reason. How unethical do you find his actions? How typical of your experience in business? Do you accept Mistler's implication that business ethics are different from personal ethics?

3. When Mistler exposes Peter Berry's betrayal of him, Peter is unrepentant, citing Mistler's mistreatment. Which man do you find more blameworthy in this broken friendship? Is either more sinned against than sinning?

4. Mistler confesses he has "ruined" Clara's life. What does he mean? Why has their marriage proved a disappointment to each? In what way does it typify the mistakes he believes he has made in life?

5. Mistler describes Mme Portes as "the only woman [he] ever loved," a woman he "never had and never lost." How do you understand his feelings for his father's mistress? Why do you suppose he has never known another love despite his many romantic opportunities?

6. How is Mistler's relationship with his father different from Sam's relationship with Mistler? How do Mistler and Sam's respective character traits inform and limit their relationship?

7. What motivates Mistler to go see Bella a second time? Why does the encounter unfold as it does?

8. How do you interpret Mistler's decision to purchase the wherry? How might we see this as a coda for his story?

9. The book's epigraph's may be translated as "Too bad about what men will lose; they'll never notice it. Everything ends well because everything ends." Mme Portes echoes this statement. How might we understand the novel in relation to this maxim?

10. Some critics have found Mistler difficult to like. How do you feel about him? How do your feelings affect your response to the book?

© Isolde Ohlbaum

ABOUT THE AUTHOR

LOUIS BEGLEY lives in New York City. His previous novels are *Wartime Lies*, *The Man Who Was Late*, *As Max Saw It*, and *About Schmidt*.